ALIETTE DE BODARD

OF CHARMS, GHOSTS
AND GRIEVANCES

ALSO BY ALIETTE DE BODARD

* available as a JABberwocky edition worldwide
† available as a JABberwocky edition in North America
^ available as a JABberwocky edition outside of North America

OF CHARMS, GHOSTS AND GRIEVANCES

A DRAGONS AND BLADES STORY

ALIETTE DE BODARD

JABberwocky Literary Agency, Inc.

Of Charms, Ghosts and Grievances
by Aliette de Bodard

This paperback edition published in 2022 by JABberwocky Literary
Agency, Inc., in association with the Zeno Agency LTD.

http://www.awfulagent.com/ebooks

Cover art © 2022 by Ravven

ISBN 978-1-625675-94-1

Up until Asmodeus spoke up, it had been an uneventful day — or, at any rate, not more eventful than usual. Thuan was visiting his family: the dynasty of shape-changing dragons that ruled the underwater kingdom of the Seine, among whom was his Second Aunt, the empress of the kingdom, and his many cousins. He and his Fallen angel husband Asmodeus had come down from the ruins of Paris, taking a much-needed break from Hawthorn, the House they jointly ruled. It was a holiday for both of them: Thuan didn't miss the committees, or the intrigues among the various magical factions within the House — or worse, the state dinners with other Fallen angels, very few of whom he actually appreciated.

Thuan's cousin had asked him to mind the children —
an offer Thuan had said yes to, because the next person
on his cousin's list had been Thuan's husband Asmodeus,
and the words "Asmodeus" and "babysitting" in the same
sentence were properly blood-curdling. Anything involv-
ing Asmodeus and patience and gentleness and diplo-
macy, in fact. It wasn't that he didn't understand children:
it was just that his idea of age-appropriate included lectures on stab-wounds and detailed explanations on how
to terrorize other children to do one's bidding. Thuan was
absolutely sure none of his aunties would approve. Worse,
they would pointedly remind him at every single family
occasion that he was the eldest in the couple and should
provide his husband with a good example.

Thuan cleaned up a lot of Asmodeus's messes, and he
didn't need extras.

So Thuan took the children to a deserted area at the
back of the citadel, on the edge of the forest of kelp that
sheltered the imperial hunting lodge, and watched them
play. They ranged from about nine to three years old, and
all knew each other; and Ai Nhi and Camille, Thuan and
Asmodeus's nieces — who had come from Hawthorn, so
that *their* parents could have a break — were busy bossing
all of them around with an ease which suggested they'd
been practicing.

It was a quiet, beautiful day: over them was the sun
of the dragon kingdom, a distant rippling orb, as if seen
through water and from a great distance. The kingdom
was underwater, its denizens water spirits, but it existed

in a bubble of its own where magic kept everyone breathing and anchored to the riverbed: the children were kicking up clouds of silt as they ran, and the huge stalks of varech bent in what might have been a current, or what might have been an invisible wind.

Asmodeus had come along: he'd spent the first half of the morning sharpening an impressive array of knives that he'd managed to secrete in his swallowtail suit. Thuan had had to shepherd the children away, because Asmodeus looked quite ready to give a lecture and a demonstration. Now Asmodeus was reading a book, lounging on a rock. He'd shrugged off his jacket, and the crisp white of his shirt shone in the wavering sunlight. His entire being appeared limned with light: the black hair with a touch of grey at the temples, which Thuan ached to run his fingers through; the rectangular tortoiseshell glasses he wore over grey-green eyes, an affectation since like all Fallen, he had perfect eyesight; his long, delicate fingers and the white gloves he always wore outside. His face was sharp, focused on his book — another of the Gothic romances he enjoyed, especially when he got to complain about the characters' surplus of scruples or lack of intelligence.

He'd offered to help and Thuan had emphatically shot that down, and Asmodeus's only answer had been a sharp, ironic smile. By evening Thuan would be worn out, and they both knew it — and Asmodeus would be sure to offer sex Thuan wouldn't even have the energy for, and to regretfully downgrade it to cuddles and tea and steamed buns. Bastard.

Thuan was focused on the three children racing each other at the edge of the group — the other four were playing shells, with Camille gleefully snatching all the ones she'd won and holding them in a chubby death-grip. The first three were a little too close to a clump of giant kelp, which meant he'd lose them if he didn't pay attention.

"Thuan," Asmodeus said. His voice was quiet, matter of fact. It was that, more than anything else, which made Thuan look up with his heart in his throat — the very idea that something was serious enough that his husband wouldn't have any sarcasm for it.

"What?"

"You have one extra child among your charges."

"I—" Thuan stopped. He stared. Things kept blurring and seizing — which in itself should have been a clue, because six children shouldn't have been that hard to tell apart. "I count six."

"No, seven. The last one is a ghost."

"Uh." Thuan stared, hard, at the seventh child, transparent and faded — they kept weaving their way between the six others, blurring between their bodies. He couldn't make out the last child's face, or their clothes, or anything, and ghosts were a serious matter. He looked for threads of *khi*-water, the natural magic of the dragon kingdom — could he weave a peachwood sword or a drum and a gong with it? How did he warn the other children to get away from the ghost without warning the ghost?

And saw, to his horror, Asmodeus walk straight up to the ghost child, kneeling to be at their level with not a care in the world. "Hello there. What's your name?"

The child stopped blurring. The temperature in the air plummeted. Asmodeus gestured for the other children to shelter behind him — which they all did, except Camille, who stuck to Asmodeus's leg with the ease of long practice. Asmodeus, with equally long practice, peeled her off, and gestured for her to join the others: Camille pouted with an "Unka" which died on her lips when she saw his face, and *dove* behind his back.

The ghost was a girl, perhaps seven or eight years of age, the same age as Ai Nhi. She had a topknot and ill-fitting clothes — not linen ones, but folded and creased paper ones, and the smell of ashes clung to her. Her eyes were silver, the light in them shimmering like molten metal.

Her mouth moved. Her lips stretched, jaw yawning wider than any human one should have done. Her teeth were white, with a network of yellowed cracks, like old celadon but without any of the fragile beauty. What came out was a thin, reedy whisper like a dying man's gasp. Asmodeus didn't flinch, but Thuan didn't like the expression on his face: it suggested he was seconds away from stabbing someone — though it wouldn't be the child. Asmodeus treated children with a mixture of fascination and extreme protectiveness.

Blood blossomed from some invisible wound in the chest, staining the clothes. Asmodeus opened his mouth, but Thuan got there first. "Show me," he said.

The child shrugged. She held out a red-stained hand — blood dripped, slow and steady, to the ground. *Ancestors, watch over me*, Thuan thought, as he grabbed it.

It was cold, but not unpleasant. The blood didn't seem to touch or stain him, and she led him, gently but firmly, out of the patch of kelp forest Ai Nhi and the other children had been playing with, and into its deeper and darker areas. Behind him, only silence, and over him, shadow; the child's feet made no noise. Thuan's hackles rose, the antlers of his dragon form shimmering into existence on his temples, just below his topknot. He didn't take on his full dragon form — the long, serpentine body with stubby arms and clawed hands, and a flowing mane in addition to the antlers — because it was too large, and Heaven only knew where he was headed and how narrow it would be. But all the same, he was wary.

The child led him to a dilapidated courtyard in a ruined complex, with huge swathes of kelp growing over scattered rocks. Thuan thought, at first, that it was a temple complex, but he soon saw that it was the ruins of something much smaller: there was only one courtyard, and no tower or large shrine. Three buildings clustered around the courtyard: unusually, not pavilions with a covered gallery and pillars at the entrance, but squat ones with rectangular doorways at the top of short flights of stairs, and no flaring roofs. Everything was covered in a thin layer of the mould that was omnipresent within the dragon kingdom, a testament to the general decay both above and under the Seine.

The ghost led him, unerringly, towards one of the buildings: a large shrine with a defaced statue of a woman. She had a soft, narrow face that must have been quite beautiful once, before robbers got into the shrine: the eyes had been gouged out and the cheeks dug into, and her hands were broken off at the wrists. Scattered offerings lay in front of her: in spite of the state of its central statue, the shrine was obviously still frequented, with incense still being burnt and fruit being laid out. There was something... haphazard about the offerings.

Too few of them, that was the issue. It was a single person bringing these, and no one else, which meant few worshippers. An isolated shrine with a functionally dying cult.

The child stopped somewhere to the left of the statue, in the shadow of its left arm. She stood, jaw still yawning impossibly wide, and pointed. "Here?" Thuan asked.

The child said nothing. She was wavering, as if in a great wind, the contours of her face blurring. Thuan walked forward, and felt something crunch under his feet.

Bones.

They were small, and scattered, and unmistakably human. Thuan knelt, raising a cloud of dust, and stared at them, trying to collect his thoughts. He wove strands of *khi*-water, letting it tremble over the floor — his spell lit up, one by one, each of the scattered bones, a host of small islands of icy blue shivering in the darkness.

"That's a lot of bones."

Thuan hadn't heard Asmodeus come in. "The children!" he said.

"At the door," Asmodeus said. "I told them not to come

in unless they wanted me to get *very* cross with them." They were clustering, uncertainly, in the door frame — Ai Nhi was holding them back, speaking urgently about Unka Asmo and how he always knew best. Trust his niece to never shut up, even in situations like these. "What do you have?"

"These," Thuan said. He gestured towards the floor. "You said there were a lot of them."

"Hmmm," Asmodeus knelt. A whiff of his perfume — bergamot and orange blossom — wafted up to Thuan. Asmodeus looked up, briefly, at the ghost, and then back at the bones. "Just very scattered. They're hers. The build matches, and I don't see extra ones. How did you die?" he said, to the child.

The child was cocking her head, as if pondering what to say.

"Asmodeus! That's hardly appropriate."

"She's dead," Asmodeus said. "And she just led you to her corpse. Don't be sentimental. Ghosts who stick around have unfinished business, do they not?"

"She could simply want a proper funeral," Thuan said.

Asmodeus's magic was trembling on the skeleton, a faint shimmering glow of Fallen radiance: a spell of reconstruction to tell him how she'd died. His face was grave, his gaze moving over the scattered bones. "There's no trace of violence. No fractured bones, no blood, and no weapon." He frowned, as the magic picked out a rib, then another. "She was slight, and the bones are too fragile. Malnourished. Very malnourished."

Thuan opened his mouth, closed it. "She died of *hunger*?"

"I think so." The anger in Asmodeus's face was visible. "Crawled here to seek refuge, to beg the protection of the immortal."

"How long ago?" The ghost was watching them, her face unreadable. She didn't look sad or angry, but then she wasn't human anymore.

"Fifty, sixty years ago? At least." Asmodeus made a stabbing gesture, and the magic snuffed itself out. "She looks like a wandering beggar. A hungry and desperate child, in the wide and wondrous dragon capital. I would guess an orphan. She wouldn't have ended up here, in such an isolated shrine, if she'd had parents or anyone watching over her." His face was stretched in that familiar smile: irony that barely masked anger.

Thuan didn't react. Truth be told, Asmodeus had a point. No one should die of hunger, and that it had happened this close to the palace was an abomination. "Do you think she wants revenge on those who neglected her? Sounds like all of them would be dead at that point." Thuan was half-minded to go have a word with them, possibly with an entire squad of imperial soldiers to get the point across.

"She doesn't feel angry to me," Asmodeus said. "Still hungry in death, perhaps?"

"She doesn't look like a hungry ghost."

Asmodeus raised an eyebrow. "How can you tell?" And, to the child, "Are you hungry? For food? For blood?

For something else?"

The child yawned, displaying those cracked teeth — her lips moved, shaping a word. She seemed to have realised neither of them could hear it, for she shook her head instead.

Since Asmodeus didn't have any knowledge of dragon kingdom ghosts, Thuan felt obliged to say, "Hungry ghosts look more unkempt. Or pulling out people's entrails and eating them, depending on how bad the hunger gets."

Asmodeus didn't look impressed, but then he'd seen worse. And done worse, quite likely. Thuan got in the next question before his husband could lead them astray. "Do you want a proper funeral?"

The child keened, a piercing sound that sent Thuan to the stone floor. She was still frantically shaking her head — clearly he'd said something wrong. "I'm sorry I maligned you—" Thuan started, ignoring Asmodeus's sarcastic smile — his husband hadn't moved, and didn't look to be bothered by the keening at all — the child screamed again, cutting him off. She squared her shoulders, finally, and pointed.

There was a single bone in a corner of the room, which looked to be a rib. Thuan wasn't an expert in bones or in bodies — he didn't have Asmodeus's casual familiarity with hurting people, thank Heaven, but there didn't seem to be anything special about the bone —

Oh.

"Wait," he said, and walked across the dusty floor, towards the darkened area. There were no other bones, which meant everything was dark. Which meant that they'd missed the obvious.

There was another corpse.

This one wasn't just bones, and there was no question they had not died a natural death. For one thing, there was too much blood.

"There's no smell," Asmodeus said. He knelt by the corpse's side, looking briefly back at the statue of the shrine. "Of blood, or of decay."

"No," Thuan said. Both he and Asmodeus had a fine sense of smell, especially for things like this. "I think it's the ghost. Or the magic in the place. Or both." Everything was saturated with *khi*-currents of water, the usual magic of the dragon kingdom and the one that Thuan wielded, like most dragons. But there was a weave on top of everything else, some kind of preservation spell — probably something to keep the offerings safe.

"Or something else," Asmodeus said.

The ghost was kneeling on Asmodeus's other side. She smiled, showing those very creepy teeth again. She looked almost... satisfied? "I'm going to make inquiries about a monk when we get back," Thuan said. "There's got to be a way we can talk to her that doesn't involve guessing."

"Mmm." Asmodeus was lifting the corpse's blood-soaked clothes. "Come here, will you?"

"What is it?" Thuan said. Up close, the corpse looked oddly inanimate: the face pale, the limbs shrunken.

"You're the expert in kingdom people. And clothes. All I can tell is that she was a fish of some kind." Fallen magic glimmered on Asmodeus's hands: he was casting another spell of reconstruction. "And that she died two days ago. Blade driven into her, a couple times: the first one went through a couple major organs and would have eventually killed her, but the second one sliced the jugular. She bled out quickly. I can't find the blade, but it was something sharp, and very thin." He looked, speculatively, at Thuan's face, and reached out to touch Thuan's topknot. "Like a slightly larger hairpin."

Thuan shook himself free. "I'm not a walking demonstration for your deductions."

"Shame." Asmodeus smiled. "I take it everyone wears hairpins here."

Thuan nodded, briskly. "All officials, and most concubines, too. Unbound hair is... mmm. Too wild."

"Ah. I did think it was going to have different connotations here than rakishly Bohemian." Asmodeus looked thoughtful. Thuan was afraid of asking what he was pondering.

Thuan peered at the corpse, for a while. "Low rank official," he said, finally. "Blowfish — look at the spines on her cheeks. These would have puffed up when she were angry." The spines in question now looked like drooping plants. "She has a patch of rank, but it's blank. A clerk in one of the outer offices, perhaps? It would explain why she was out here." He frowned. Come to think of here, why was she here at all? The shrine was deserted. "What do you want?" he asked the child. "A proper funeral for her?"

A hesitant shake of her head, followed by a yes. So a

funeral, but not the only thing.

"Revenge," Asmodeus said, sharply and bleakly. "Someone killed that woman. In front of you?"

The child nodded, twice — one for each question. Her face was grave. Thuan couldn't really read the expression on it: too much remove from him, and her features subtly wavered. "Look," he said, "There are protocols and people. We really shouldn't—" but Asmodeus cut him off.

"We'll look into it. You have my word."

He was bored again, and wanted something to keep him busy in the middle of citadel politics — and fewer things kept him busier than vengeance. Or perhaps he was simply angry, because he had once been leader of the Court of Birth, responsible for the safety of all of House Hawthorn's children, and old habits died hard. Thuan wasn't sure which. "We need to talk about this," he said.

A shrug, from Asmodeus. "Not here." He was standing up, brushing his hands. "I've seen all I need to see. Have a look, and then we'll leave."

"Asmodeus—" Thuan stared at the ghost, who stared levelly at him — and then at the doorway, where the children were still clustering. "I see. The children. You're not usually so considerate."

"There's too much unknown in this place," Asmodeus said. He was on edge, then, and no wonder. He always was, when going into the dragon kingdom. It was Thuan's family home, but not a place where he held any power or influence — and in Asmodeus's world, power, and the threats it allowed him to make, was what underpinned everything. "I want them back in the citadel."

Asmodeus headed, purposefully, towards the children clustered in the doorway. Ai Nhi, detaching herself from the group, ran towards him, and stopped. She wanted a hug, and was well aware she probably wouldn't get one: Asmodeus didn't really do affection that way. Asmodeus made a gesture Thuan couldn't see, and Ai Nhi buried his face against his chest. The other children clustered around him, vying for attention.

All right, very much on edge then.

And then, Thuan realised with dawning horror that among the children was the ghost. He hadn't seen her move. "Asmodeus!" he said.

Asmodeus looked down, at the ghost child. An expansive shrug. "We did need to bring her too, didn't we? She's a material witness."

A ghost in the imperial citadel — how much paperwork and how many explanations and justifications would Thuan have to give to Second Aunt and to all his cousins; how many lectures would he get from concerned aunties to stop mingling with death as it was bad for him, with a sideways look that included Asmodeus in the death group. "We can't just bring a ghost with us!"

But Asmodeus had already walked off. Typical.

"You want an exorcist." Hong Chi's voice was flat. She barely looked up from the tray of tea things in front of her: red clay teapot, balled tea leaves on a plate, warm water in a cracked celadon pitcher. By the looks of it, Thuan had interrupted her on her break.

"Well, yes," Thuan said, with the brightest smile he could muster. "But not, per se, for an exorcism. More... a technical problem."

Hong Chi was Thuan's cousin and head of the Embroidered Guard, the palace citadel's service of spies and internal security. Her office was huge, its ceiling awash with carvings, dotted with diamond-shaped alcoves where various scrolls waited for her attention. Everything smelled of mould and some kind of unpleasant algae: the carvings were for the most part broken off or eroded, and the scrolls had grey and brown flecks growing on them. Hong Chi said, "A technical problem. In the palace. That requires an exorcist."

Thuan knew that expression well: it suggested she was indulging him only for family's sake, instead of giving him a (well-deserved, from her point of view) lecture.

The last Thuan had seen of said technical problem, she had been with Asmodeus: his husband had been handling bedtime, sitting in the middle of the children's bedroom, reading from a bloodcurdling story to an audience of Ai Nhi, Camille, and a flickering ghost. The ghost's face was hard to read, but her bloodshot eyes were half-lidded, her fang-filled mouth relaxed and turned upwards: a half-sleepy smile. Asmodeus was even harder to read, but Thuan thought he looked pleased, and not a little bit smug. Trust his husband to feel at ease with a ghost. "Yes," Thuan said. He smiled brightly again. His lips hurt from too much stretching. "Also, we're going to need a magistrate. One of the palace court ones."

Hong Chi's face was still flat, but it was clear it had required an effort to keep it so. She laid both hands on her desk. Like everything in the citadel, it had been patched: the lacquer had cracked and been painted over many times, and mould still clung to its corner. "Still to do with your technical problem?"

"Well, tangentially related, but yes."

A pause. Hong Chi sighed, massaging her forehead. Her dragon antlers were coming out at her temples, and so was a scattering of iridescent scales on her forehead. She'd expertly hid the patch of rot on her left cheek with some ceruse, but stress was making it stand out. "All right, out with it. I asked you two to babysit, not to go murder someone. The brief was, I believe, quite explicit on the matter. The only reason why I'm being very calm about this is because I know you returned all the children safely."

"You know we'd never harm children. Or allow them to be harmed."

"I do," Hong Chi said. "I'm worried about what you'll do to people who try to harm them."

That was... not inaccurate. Asmodeus had very strong ideas about protecting the people in his charge, and he applied these double or triple to children. Thuan was less stab-happy, but no way he was going to let someone hurt children on his watch. "We didn't kill anyone."

He could see the "yet" forming on Hong Chi's lips. To

forestall it, he said, "There's a body. And a ghost."

Hong Chi's stare, reptilian and hard, could have melted metal. He amended. "It's two different people." It was not going to make things better, but he was a scholar to the end: accuracy mattered. "And someone most definitely killed the body. With extreme prejudice. The ghost saw it happen."

Hong Chi stared at him. "Extreme prejudice. Is that your opinion, or your husband's? His idea of 'extreme prejudice' has me extremely worried."

"I don't think Asmodeus has expressed an opinion," Thuan said, carefully. "But there's a blowfish clerk lying dead in an isolated shrine, some distance from the court. Stabbed a couple of times." He described, as best as he could, the place the children had been playing — and watched Hong Chi's face harden, the patches of grey scales on her cheeks flickering into existence.

"The Anemone Immortal's shrine," she said, flatly.

"I don't know who that is." The word "tiên" Hong Chi had used referred to someone who had ascended and got magical powers beyond the *khi*-currents due to meritorious acts. "Is she at court?" Unlikely; most immortals shunned the company of their former equals.

"No." It sounded like Hong Chi was going to add something, but Thuan got there first.

"Anemone?"

"The story goes that an official riding in her palanquin saw a lady picking up anemones by the side of the road. When the palanquin passed by, the lady called out 'hail to the bearer of the White March Beast patch'. The official was puzzled, as she wasn't of the second rank and not entitled to that patch of rank yet. But when she called out to her, the lady vanished. The official went back to the palace, and within a couple of days, she was promoted to the second rank. She built the shrine to honour the lady by the roadside — it became a place where officials prayed for advancement and continued success at the court."

"You said the Anemone Immortal wasn't at court. I take it she hasn't been seen at her shrine for a while?"

Hong Chi made a face. "No. There's a reason why you've never heard of her. Her cult was active in the time of... our grandmother, and then it petered out long before you came back to court. She disappeared around the same time."

A common enough story. "She was ashamed and fled from her worshippers."

"Probably," Hong Chi said. "It was more than a hundred years ago. Ancient history."

"Mmm. Why would anybody go there, then?"

"I don't know," Hong Chi said. "Or why anyone would stab her. Or who she is, really. But I'm planning to look into it. Where is the ghost now?"

"Ah." Thuan said, smiling as brightly as he could — bracing himself for Hong Chi's reaction. "You're not going to like this."

"Asmodeus?" Thuan opened the double doors of their quarters, and found Asmodeus in the children's bedroom, sitting in a chair, a book in his lap. He wasn't reading, though: his attention was on the children sleeping huddled against each other in the bed behind him. It was an adult bed under a high canopy, the two gashes in its embroidered brocade painstakingly repaired. The sheets were spread straight over the wooden surface of the bed, the way they always were in the citadel. Neither Thuan nor Asmodeus minded but Ai Nhi, who had complained about the lack of mattress, had piled up cushions and was sleeping on them with her plush toy snake. She was in dragon shape, wrapped around Camille, who at five years old was sucking her thumb and clutching her mouldy blanket. The ghost was lying down on the bed a little away from them both, eyes closed — was she sleeping, too?

When Asmodeus saw the unfamiliar dragon trailing behind Thuan, his hand moved — and came back holding a knife he didn't bother to hide.

Thuan sighed. "Can you put that away?"

"Maybe." Asmodeus's face was jewel-hard. "Who's your friend?" The accent on the word made it clear they were most definitely not *his* friend.

"This is Quang Thu. I didn't find an exorcist, but Hong Chi sent her to help. She's a court palace magistrate and she's got some knowledge of ghosts."

Quang Thu was rail thin, with a shaved head — she looked like she'd wandered out of a monastery, except that she also wore an embroidered patch on a roughly-dyed purple tunic. She stared, for a while, at the bed — and then back at Asmodeus. "Honoured to meet you." She sounded cautious, but not unfriendly. "You said you found a body."

"Yes. It's in that ruined shrine," Asmodeus said. He still held the knife, but his hand had relaxed a fraction: he no longer looked as though he was going to stab Quang Thu with it. Small mercies. "You're free to go see it."

"In the morning. The ghost first." Quang Thu stared at the ghost — said ghost hadn't moved. She was lying on the bed next to Camille, ghostly shape flickering as if in an invisible wind. "She is genuinely sleeping. How did you do that?"

Asmodeus smiled. "Bedtime stories. Everyone sleeps once they're over. It's the rule."

Quang Thu's face went through an interesting set of expressions. "Ghosts usually don't. Unless you have some talent with exorcism or a personal link to them." She pulled a high-backed chair, sat down. "Tell me about how you found the body."

When Asmodeus was done — his description was grave, factual, clinical — Quang Thu stared, for a while, at the broken dragon carvings of the ceiling. "That's a very ugly murder. Did the child witness it?"

"Yes," Thuan said.

"And has anybody reassured the child?"

"She's dead."

"Which changes nothing about my question."

Asmodeus smiled. Thuan could tell he approved of Quang Thu but was never, per se, ever going to get around to admitting it her. "As I said. Bedtime stories."

Thuan said, "She's trying to speak, but we can't understand what she's saying."

"You wouldn't." Quang Thu stared at the ghost again. "Most ghosts don't linger, either. And they certainly don't become untethered from the place of their death that way. She's unusual. You said she died of hunger?"

"In all likelihood," Asmodeus said. "It's an ugly way to go." He was angry again. "I'm impressed she hasn't started killing people in the capital for looking the other way while she was slowly starving to death."

Quang Thu smiled. Thuan could tell Asmodeus had passed some kind of test. "Not everyone is angry in death." She sighed. "I could tell you she shouldn't have died that way, but you know it already, don't you?"

"And is anything going to be done about it?"

Quang Thu laughed. "Your husband has already had words with at least three different officials about making sure the beggars in the capital got fed, and to get those orphan kids the imperial guard could find to orphanages and schools."

Thuan reddened. "Look," he started.

"Good," Asmodeus nodded, and backed down by a few centimeters. "Late and barely acceptable, but good." It was clear he was talking about the court, and not Thuan. "Thuan really shouldn't have had to remind you."

"Can we keep the conversation on the ghost?" Thuan asked. He was the centre of both their attentions and felt terminally embarrassed about it.

"If you want. The ghost wants revenge," Asmodeus said.

"Justice," Thuan said, and Asmodeus gave him a *look*. *Are you really that naive?* "Quang Thu is a magistrate. We're not here for retribution."

"We're not, though I don't want to presume what the ghost wants. But even revenge — or justice — on behalf of someone else isn't usually enough for ghosts to linger." Quang Thu rose, pulling out a series of things from her sleeves: three silver coins, a pile of papers, a chopstick. She put them on the mahogany table next to the bed. "I'm going to need a volunteer."

"A volunteer for what?" Thuan asked.

"A little bit of a painful experience." Quang Thu flicked her fingers: wind rose in the room, and a faint music started — no, not music, merely a song that half sounded like a mourning lament. The papers unfolded: they weren't written reports, but fine lacework that slowly twisted back on itself again and again, until it became a three-lobed paper arch, like the doors of a ghostly temple or palace. "Ghosts pass on, unless they find sustenance."

"Sustenance," Thuan said, flatly. Entrails and organs and blood. "You mean feeding on someone."

"Yes."

"You said painful," Asmodeus said.

"Yes," Quang Thu said. "Ghosts that can hang on for that long are hungry and driven. That will become part of you. The ghost's life will be entwined with yours."

Thuan opened his mouth to say he'd do it, and found it sealed. Magic — Asmodeus's magic — was holding it shut. "Asmodeus!" he tried to say, but his husband smiled, all sharp teeth. "Behave," he mouthed, before turning to Quang Thu.

"What should I do?" he asked.

Asmodeus! Thuan tried to move — the magic moved, too, holding the rest of his body immobile as Quang Thu put the chopstick just next to the sleeping ghost's lips. The air felt like tar.

They were going to have words when this was over. So many words.

"Put the coins under the arches," Quang Thu said. Asmodeus's face betrayed nothing but mild curiosity — his magic still holding Thuan's body in an iron grip, though the touch on Thuan's lips was now an insistent caress. Asmodeus lined up the coins, his face creased as if considering a particularly thorny problem — and brought them, one after the other, under the arches. As each coin slid in a small tremor shook the room — and with the last one the palace doors shivered, and collapsed, just as the music was abruptly cut off. The ghost jolted awake, mouth open in a soundless scream — just as Asmodeus fell to his knees.

The magic holding Thuan vanished abruptly. "Asmodeus!" He knelt by his husband, stared into a white, drawn face that instantly composed itself into the old, familiar, sarcastic mask.

"The child first," Asmodeus snapped. And, when Thuan didn't move, he pulled himself up — only the faint faltering betraying the pain he was labouring under — and moved onto the bed, to hold the ghost against his chest. "You didn't say it would harm her," he snarled.

"It didn't. It'll pass," Quang Thu said. She hadn't moved. She looked grey and exhausted. "Consider it... necessary pain."

By the looks of it, Asmodeus was considering whether to inflict entirely unnecessary pain as retribution — and Thuan couldn't even feel sorry about it.

"He's right," he said. "You could have warned us. You could have woken the children up, too."

"The *other* children," Asmodeus said, without looking up.

Thuan was having trouble thinking of the ghost as a child.

"I didn't expect it to make quite so much noise," Quang Thu said.

Asmodeus was whispering something Thuan couldn't quite make out, rocking the ghost back and forth. The ghost's face was smoothing itself out — not just quieter, but completely emptying itself of features until nothing was left but smooth skin. It was altogether too creepy: Thuan tried not to look. "Let's move somewhere else," he said. Quang Thu shrugged, and moved into the reception room.

Thuan lingered, to see Asmodeus lay down a sleeping ghost on the bed. When he looked up again, his usual mask had slipped back into place. Thuan wasn't fooled: anything that had Asmodeus fall to his knees was all but unbearable pain.

Pain Asmodeus had taken on himself without consulting Thuan.

"What did you think you were doing?" Thuan asked, as Asmodeus caught up with him on the way out of the bedroom.

A smile. "Preventing you from making a bad decision."

"Because it would hurt?"

"Because you're too soft, dragon prince." Asmodeus's hand lingered on Thuan's nape, gently drawing circles on his skin. Thuan shivered.

"I can bear pain."

"You can." Asmodeus's face was creased in that particular expression again — barely controlled anger. "But you don't have to."

Oh. Thuan opened his mouth, closed it. "We could have *discussed* it."

"In the middle of the night, in the children's bedroom? Most emphatically not."

"You can't keep running away from conversations you don't feel like having!"

"Try me." Asmodeus's face was hard. He moved into the reception room where Quang Thu was waiting. It was the widest room in their quarters, open on one side to a courtyard containing a skeletal, ghost-white coral that was obviously in decline. A long, narrow table with high-backed mahogany chairs held a pile of books they'd brought over from Hawthorn, and their tea cups. Thuan had insisted with Asmodeus that he be the one to brew the tea: Asmodeus took his black, strong, and frequently overbrewed, whereas Thuan's taste ran to the more delicate and flowery teas — the ones that were all but impossible to find in a kingdom where the least of the crops tasted of rot. He'd settled for some semi-oxidized tea — which, even flecked with mould and dubious underwater fungi, was better than the strong black Asmodeus kept insisting was drinkable.

Asmodeus walked straight to where Quang Thu was standing. "Now tell me why any of this had to be done now."

Quang Thu grimaced. "I'm sorry. I didn't expect this ritual to be so complicated, or so noisy. The child shouldn't have woken up. As to why — the body isn't going to get deader, but ghosts become unmoored if they're not anchored or feeding on people. And this one left the place of her death, which weakens her further."

"You said it was going to be a painful experience," Thuan said. "What happens after it's over?"

Quang Thu's face didn't move. "I'll set her free from you, and presumably she'll return to where she died."

Which was an interesting way of not answering the question. "You said her leaving the place of her death was unusual," Thuan said.

"She's very strong," Asmodeus said. He'd pulled a chair to sit in, and his cup of tea had mysteriously appeared in his hand. By the way he was gripping it, he was in pain. Thuan moved, gently and unobtrusively laid his hands on Asmodeus's shoulders. Asmodeus's body relaxed a fraction. He said nothing. Obviously. To do so would have been to admit weakness.

Quang Thu pursed her lips. "I don't think there's anything we can do until morning anyway. Until the child wakes up, and assuming she's willing to talk."

"How is she going to talk?" Asmodeus asked. "Is there some kind of magical link?"

Quang Thu laughed. "No. But you don't need words to talk. We're going to do this the old-fashioned way: ask her questions and see what she says. But not now."

She was a ghost, not a child. She didn't *actually* need to sleep. "We could wake her—" Thuan started, and Asmodeus's shoulders bunched up under his hands, his husband's face tilting up to glare at him.

"No. She's been scared enough as it is already."

"There is no hurry," Quang Thu said, smoothly. "I'm going to get a look at the body. Let's see each other at breakfast."

After she was gone, Asmodeus relaxed a fraction — which meant the pain he was trying to hide just became more visible. Which was bad. Asmodeus's tolerance for pain was high. "How bad are you?" Thuan asked.

An ironic smile. "No worse than I was in the hawthorn grove."

Thuan remembered Asmodeus, kneeling bloodied and broken on churned earth, back in House Hawthorn. He'd almost died, clinging on to life only because of his determination to defend House Hawthorn and his dependents at any cost. "It took you *months* to recover from the grove."

Asmodeus's face was a careful mask. "A pleasant hospital stay, was it not. Iaris enjoyed fussing over me."

He'd been in bed, first in the Hawthorn hospital and then in his bedroom. Fallen healed themselves faster than dragons, and without any need for conscious healing spells. Asmodeus had been so badly injured he'd required litres of transfused blood — so many Thuan had lost track. "I didn't enjoy the fussing," Thuan said, shortly. "You're a terrible patient."

Asmodeus smiled. It was wide and wounding. "In all fairness, you did contribute to landing me in the sick bed."

"Self-defence," Thuan said, shortly. Their relationship had started with an arranged marriage and them at each other's throats. "You did try to kill me."

"A detail," Asmodeus said. "Fortunately, our relationship has improved greatly since then, wouldn't you say?" He bent, giving Thuan a slow and forceful kiss that temporarily silenced him, Fallen magic filling Thuan with a pleasant, roilling warmth.

"You're impossible," Thuan said, when Asmodeus pulled away. He ran a hand over his husband's sharp cheek, unwilling to let go of the warmth.

"That, too. We did bring a cane, didn't we?" Asmodeus asked.

That did nothing to reassure Thuan. He dropped his hand. "Yes. The one with the silver hunting hound pommel. Please stop making me anxious by deflecting."

"I can bear it," Asmodeus said. He grimaced. "Not for long, so we'd better find out who killed that official fast.

Did you notice Quang Thu dodged your question?"

"The one about what would happen to the ghost? Yes," Thuan said. "I'm more worried about you than the ghost."

"I can see that," Asmodeus said. "But I can take care of myself. The ghost, no."

"She's a *ghost!*"

"She's a child."

"Is this about the Court of Birth in Hawthorn? You're not its leader anymore. And the ones that died back then weren't your fault."

A silence. Asmodeus stared at him. His face was jewel-hard again. "Everyone who dies under my watch is my failure. Don't you know this?"

"She's dead already!"

"She's conscious. And sentient. You're a dragon. Are you going to tell me you're afraid of ghosts?"

"Yes," Thuan said. "Absolutely."

"Why?"

"Because they're ghosts! Because they can kill you. Tear you apart and eat your guts. Or follow you home and haunt you until you go mad."

"And does it look like she's doing any of that?"

"That doesn't change who she is!"

A silence again, but this one was charged. "Your lack of care for someone who needs it is disappointing."

"I'm not—" Thuan opened his month, closed it. He took a deep breath. "Fine. Let's not have this argument now."

An ironic, wounding smile. "Walking away from a

conversation you don't feel like having?"

"That's not — let's go to bed, Asmodeus."

"Gladly."

They fell asleep by each other's side in their common bed, with the silence between them like a drawn sword.

"Unka Thuan! Unka Thuan!" Thuan woke up, bleary-eyed, to Camille jumping up and down on the bed, the wood trembling with each of her leaps. Ai Nhi had sneaked in and was curling against his body. Asmodeus — he couldn't see his husband anywhere, but the memory of the argument they'd had the day was still vivid. "Stop jumping. I'm worried you'll break the bed."

"I won't!" Camille said, proudly and with the utter lack of logic of a five-year-old.

"I'm worried," Thuan said, firmly. "So stop it."

Ai Nhi made a small contented noise, and snuggled closer to him.

"Child. Did you sleep well?"

"I had nightmares," Ai Nhi said, grimacing. "Where is the ghost?"

Thuan's brain caught up. "The ghost." He was going to need a whole lot more tea, and possibly a whole bowl of noodle soup. "Let's go see, shall we?"

The ghost was sitting by Asmodeus's side in the reception room, her hands hovering over the bowl of fruit. Her face was a sickly pallor, her eyes gleaming like molten metal. She was wearing actual clothes: by the looks of it, one of Ai Nhi's white bloused tops and its matching short skirt, a sky-blue one with three black lines near the hem. Her long hair was now in a loose topknot, with most of it falling down her back. The mixture of domesticity and stomach-wrenching horror was one Thuan was having a lot of trouble with — any moment now, he expected the ghost to leap for his throat or stomach or both.

Asmodeus was showing the ghost the inside of a dragon fruit — a border of purple, and glistening black seeds on a stark white background. She seemed fascinated — her mouth yawning wide, with her sharp, cracked teeth opening only a fraction. She reached out, fingers lengthening into sharp points, piercing the fruit. Juice welled up, clear at first and then turning into the red of blood — she brought her fingers to her mouth and gently sucked on them, with the same casual ease she'd drink blood from a living being. Thuan's hand tightened on Ai Nhi's shoulder. "Be careful," he said. Ai Nhi looked at him, puzzled.

"This is Lan," Asmodeus said. He said it with the proper Viet accentuation. His grasp of Thuan's native language, after six years of marriage, was now good enough he could conduct most of the everyday conversations.

"Lan," Thuan said, slowly and with as little affect as he could. Orchid. "That's her name?"

"She spelled it for me," Asmodeus said. He watched the ghost with something very much like fondness. His face, though, was still drawn in pain. "You're not coping with it," Thuan said, flatly.

"Not now." The voice Asmodeus used was imperious, the same one that sent grown people scurrying for exits before he could find his knives. Thuan — who'd been married to him for six years now — wasn't supposed to be scared of that voice, but something in its steel caught him, too, and for a brief moment fear spiked through him. For a brief moment he *absolutely* believed Asmodeus would harm him, too. And wouldn't he, if Asmodeus thought he was threatening the ghost? "You'll scare Lan. Not to mention Ai Nhi or Camille."

Ai Nhi threw a worried glance between them. She settled down, grabbing a rambutan from the fruit basket — it was made of woven kelp, and it was also the only thing in the room that looked new and not in need of repairs. "Oh, look, lil'sis, they have the hairy things you like!"

"Chom chom," Camille said in Viet, nodding sagely. "Give."

For a moment there was nothing else but the sound of munching. Lan stabbed the dragon fruit, repeatedly, making content noises. She turned to Asmodeus and made a sound that only vaguely sounded like a dying man's scream. Asmodeus nodded. "You can have another fruit," he said.

It was utterly surreal. Thuan settled for, "She can't be getting the blood from the fruit."

"She's not." It was Quang Thu, standing in the doorway. Her gaze took in the children — she nodded, briefly to each of them. Camille nodded with her mouth full.

Ai Nhi hastily dropped the fried roll she was chewing

and bowed. "Elder aunt."

Quang Tu nodded, accepting the bow. She came in and pulled a chair. It made a high-pitched noise on the cracked tiles of the floor. "My name is Quang Tu. I'm a friend of your uncles. That looks like a good breakfast."

So Hong Chi had briefed her. Good.

"Want one?" Camille said, holding out a rambutan.

Thuan fought to take the conversation back to the essentials. "You said she wasn't getting the blood from the fruit."

"No. The fruit isn't where she's drawing her sustenance from." Quang Thu stared at Asmodeus, who stared back at her. His lips curled into an ironic smile.

She was feeding from Asmodeus. Thuan saw red. "You never said—"

"I should have thought it was obvious." Asmodeus grabbed a pair of kim giao wood chopsticks — they were topped with silver carvings, except the silver had tarnished. He dipped them into the bowl of noodle soup in front of him. "Beef and tripes. Very sensible idea to replenish one's blood."

"This isn't tenable!"

"And yet you'd blithely have volunteered for it." Asmodeus snorted. He was still angry then. Or weak. Neither of which would make him less annoying or less wounding: he had a predator's unerring instinct for which words would hurt most, and — in his current state — none of the restraints that usually kept him controlled.

Better get the children out of range of the talk they

were going to have, then. "Ai Nhi?" Thuan asked.

"Unka Thuan?"

"Why don't you and Camille go draw the tree in the courtyard?" The courtyard in question was within their chambers, and Asmodeus and Thuan had heavily warded it when they'd arrived. The children would be quite safe there. Not that anyone would dare snatch them from Thuan and Asmodeus, or at least not anyone with common sense.

Ai Nhi's gaze narrowed. "Lan—"

"Is going to be safe, but we need to have a word with her. I promise."

Ai Nhi glanced from Asmodeus to Thuan, and then nodded. "Come on," she said.

It took a couple of tries — Camille wasn't feeling enthusiastic — but at length both children were gone, bickering about who was getting the pencils, and they were alone. Silence spread — awkward and uncomfortable.

Quang Thu sighed. "I saw the body."

"And?"

"Not much more than you'd already seen." A scritching noise at the door, like a small crab. Quang Thu cocked her head, but the sound had vanished.

"Do you know who she is?"

"Yes. Thai Ha, an official of the second rank in the Palace Provisions Commissions. She oversaw the supplies of tea to the princes and the high officials."

"And what was she doing in a deserted temple?" Thuan remembered the offerings askew on the altar.

"Worshipping for success?"

A sigh from Quang Thu. "Thai Ha was ambitious. The post of Chief Commissioner had become vacant, and it was being heavily contested."

So she'd gone to a half-forgotten shrine, chasing a legend. "She wanted every chance on her side," Thuan said. "How come she knew about the Anemone Immortal?" The cult had died down, Hong Chi had said.

"Her parents were imperial archivists. It's quite probable she found the legend in a book somewhere, and thought it could give her an edge."

Which didn't much help, did it. "How many other suspects does that make?"

"The entire department," Quang Thu said. "Well. Every overseer."

Thuan tried to remember how many people were involved. Five? Six?

"We're going to need names," Asmodeus said. "And descriptions. Lan can probably tell us who it was."

"Here," Quang Thu said, slipping a folded piece of paper on the table. "These are the useful parties. It's not just overseers but also the supporters—" She paused.

"Is something wrong?" Thuan started, and then stopped, because Asmodeus had dropped the chopsticks, and whipped out a pair of knives.

"At the door," he said, curtly. And then something heavy and powerful pushed against the wards in the courtyard, shattering them. All the currents of *khi*-water in the room went haywire.

Thuan pushed his chair back. "I'm getting the children. Get Lan and Quang Thu."

He didn't pause to see what was happening, because the wards were down, and they didn't have much time.

Thuan ran. In the courtyard, Ai Nhi had put Camille behind her: she was holding a dagger not much bigger than Thuan's fists in a steady grip, and her antlers were now visible on either side of her face.

"Unka Thuan?"

Thuan looked up. Dark silhouettes hung on the roofs around the courtyard, over the faded longevity tiles — as he watched, they unfolded, lengthening. Dragons — no, not dragons, but paper streams, like the ones Quang Thu had used to build her paper palace. They dove towards Thuan and the children.

"Don't let them touch you," Thuan said, sharply. He didn't know what would happen, but he doubted it would be good. He wove a loose network of *khi*-water around them, a protective circle to give them some time.

Ai Nhi was shaking — she was about to lose control over her shape, and that wasn't going to be helpful: she wasn't large enough to carry Camille for more than a few moments. He needed — he could go full dragon, but then he'd need a way out of the courtyard and the charms were currently blocking his exit.

The first paper streamer struck Thuan's circle, and the *khi*-water just *crumpled*, decomposing.

Wait.

What.

This was emphatically very very bad.

Another of the paper streamers whipped in the breeze, making straight for Ai Nhi. Thuan threw his hand across her, and the streamer fastened on it instead.

It wasn't paper. It just... it was sharp and burning and it kept burrowing inside his skin, and it hurt and it hurt, ancestors, he could hardly focus on anything but the pain — his other hand came up, trying to scratch it off, but half the paper fastened on it instead, and that burnt too.

"Unka Thuan!"

"Don't touch me!" he said, flailing — seeing, through a haze of red, Ai Nhi dance out of his grasp. He struggled to stand. Asmodeus — where was Asmodeus? The children should run to him...

There was a sound like a dying man screaming, and the paper streamers froze and fell to the paved floor in an ungainly heap, as if the life had been drained out of them. Including the ones on Thuan's hands.

"Your hand," Ai Nhi said.

Thuan glanced at it — saw bone poking out through a wound across his palm that felt like it was cleaving his hand in two halves. "Later." He looked up, trying to find the source of the scream —

Ah.

Lan stood on the steps at the courtyard's entrance, her mouth wide open, still screaming. Asmodeus — his shirt and jacket covered in blood — ran behind her, Quang Thu, pale and shaking, by his side. And behind them, people — they looked distantly like palace guards, but something about them was off — the wrong clothes, the wrong attitude?

Thuan *changed*, shifting from human to dragon— hovering slightly above the paper streamers on the ground. Not that it would help much, if they sprang to life again. Ai Nhi and Camille clambered onto the spines of his back, followed by Quang Thu.

Asmodeus pushed Lan towards him — Lan was shaking her head, mouth still open in that scream. Asmodeus made a short, stabbing gesture. Thuan caught only the edges of his words — "you most definitely don't want to see me cross" — and then Lan was on him, and Asmodeus too, and he took off, slowly and ponderously, just as the papers fluttered upwards again, hungering for them all.

"What in the ten hells was that?" he asked, shaking.

"Good grip on that knife," Asmodeus said, appreciatively, to Ai Nhi. "The blade is a bit small."

"I couldn't hide a larger knife," Ai Nhi said. Thuan could imagine the pout. "Besides, Unka Thuan gets upset with sharp objects."

"Unka Thuan believes in talking to people." Asmodeus's usual sarcasm was muted. "Those paper things and those guards didn't really seem receptive to that approach."

Thuan cut him off before he could get going. "I'm not getting upset, in these specific circumstances." Thuan was still shaking, and his front legs hurt, and didn't seem to be healing at all. He felt raw and cranky, and utterly unsuited to reassure or steady anyone. "I'm a little busy getting upset at whoever sent those paper things our way. Whatever they are."

"Exorcists' charms," Quang Thu said.

To silence a ghost. "That paper with the names of the suspects—" Thuan said.

"I have it," Quang Thu said. "Do you want to see it?"

"Not while flying. But it looks like someone is trying to silence Lan as a witness."

Quang Thu's voice was shaking. "That many charms means someone very powerful. They don't take long to make, not with this kind of single-minded purpose, but still."

Great. They'd need to ask Lan for more details about the murderer when they landed and managed to communicate with her. Quang Thu had not been very clear on how they were going to manage that at all, but they'd find a way. "Any ideas who is doing this?" Thuan asked.

He tried to scan the roofs, looking for a place large enough to land. The citadel was huge, a maze of buildings connected by courtyards and larger spaces, spreading all the way from the Midday Gate to the Inner Quarters of the Empress and the Six Chambers where the concubines lived — and currently every single destination felt too exposed and too much of a risk. The gardens, perhaps? His grandmother's private palace? No, too many people. His gut feeling was that they'd want somewhere quiet. There.

One of the larger courtyards, a deserted one near the

former palace of his great-grandmother: there was a large pond filled with coral and elegant drawings of mother-of-pearl, and a small lacquered pavilion with mould clinging to its tiles.

He didn't land so much as flop, ungainly, the cracked tiles of the floor digging into the soft soft of his belly like claws. Ai Nhi slid down his tail, laughing as she landed. "Come on, lil'sisters," she said, to Camille and Lan. Asmodeus joined her, shielding his hand against the underwater light above them. Blood dripped from his shirt and jacket. His eyes narrowed. "Thuan?"

"Yes." Thuan was trying to get his shape under control. "I'm going to need a moment."

"You don't have it," Asmodeus said, sharply.

"Don't be so unpleasant—" Thuan started. And then he saw the paper charms coming out of the pond, fluttering downwards from the pavilion's rafters. "Child!" he screamed to Ai Nhi.

"Bad things are back," Camille said. She tried to move off Thuan. Someone — probably Quang Thu — grabbed her. Asmodeus sheltered Ai Nhi — who was trying to reach for the knife in her pocket, before Asmodeus helped steady her hand.

"Go! Now!"

Thuan lifted off just as the paper charms swirled around them. They had turned the red of the blood on Asmodeus's shirt, and they glinted in the afternoon light, a thoroughly unnecessary reminder of how deeply they could cut. This time, though, the charms rose with them

— a cloud of them in front of him — a moment's beat, and then they were entangled in his mane, burrowing towards his skin.

No.

They were going to bite into his skull, split it open.

No. He shook himself, again and again, but nothing seemed to dislodge them.

"Don't move. On second thought—" Asmodeus's magic grabbed him, held his head immobile. Thuan opened his mouth to protest, found that this, too was held — thrashed against his restraints, just as a blast of Fallen magic went straight into his mane, singeing his skull.

He tried to howl but the vice of Asmodeus's magic swallowed up his scream, and the Fallen magic kept dancing in his hair as burnt fragments fell around him. When he finally broke free, sweating, there were no paper charms left, only cinders.

"Don't thank me." Asmodeus's voice was smug.

Everything ached, from the cuts on his legs to the Fallen magic still smouldering in his hair. "You really need to stop holding me in a magical stranglehold whenever you want me to not move."

"Duly noted. And with you flying and moving as you fly, I most certainly couldn't aim magic with enough accuracy to get the paper charms but not set your face on fire. I hadn't thought you preferred getting burnt, or cut open to the bone." A snort. "We've had this discussion. Don't be so keen to volunteer to get hurt."

"You saw—?"

"Your forelegs? It's hard not to see. And they're not healing."

Thuan winced. "I'd rather not think about it."

A shrug. "A luxury. Granted, for now."

They both knew it was going to become a problem, and fast.

"What now?" Quang Thu asked. Her voice was slight and exhausted.

"I'm getting us somewhere out of the palace," Thuan said, weaving his way out of the citadel and towards the coral cliffs on the north side of the capital. "Hopefully the exorcist won't follow us here."

His brain caught up, and he realised that Lan hadn't moved at all since she'd climbed on his back. He twisted, maw going over his shoulder. She was unconscious. "What's wrong with Lan?"

Asmodeus held her in his lap. Her hair had spilled out of the topknot, a flood of black against the matching black of Asmodeus's trousers. He looked sallow. "She's been unconscious since we landed in the second courtyard."

"One of those things swiped at her," Ai Nhi said. "Unka Asmo, whose blood is on your shirt?"

"The guards'." Asmodeus pursed his lips, looking thoughtful. "I think. I don't think it's mine."

"You don't think?" Thuan asked, horrified.

"Being Lan's anchor makes it hard to work out if the pain is coming from physical wounds." It was said utterly matter-of-factly, as if it didn't count at all. As if he wasn't being drained of his life-force to sustain a ghost.

"Asmodeus!"

"Behave." Asmodeus's voice was sharp. "We can take stock of injuries after we land. And that definitely includes yours, dragon prince." He managed to make it sound like a threat.

"Well," Asmodeus said, "That's certainly a change of scenery."

"Behave," Thuan said.

"I see no reason why."

They were in an abandoned shrine. Not the Anemone Immortal's, as that was likely to be swarming with more paper charms, but another one at the foot of the coral cliffs, little more than a three-arch gate, a courtyard and a building with a wide pillared entrance and a sloping roof, opening into the cliffside. Pale, dying coral had colonised the tiles of the roof, and the courtyard was filled with mouldy rubble, a mixture of rocks and coral. It smelled half of rot, half of faded incense.

They'd been on the ground for five whole minutes and nothing had attacked them yet, which was a great improvement on previous minutes. Quang Thu was leaning against one of the mouldy lacquered pillars of the temple's entrance, obviously struggling to catch her breath — and by the look of shock on her face, dealing with a fair amount of internal turmoil.

"Not here, lil'sis," Ai Nhi said to Camille, who was cheerfully wandering inside the shrine's deserted interior.

"There might be ghosts."

"And God forbid we have more ghosts," Asmodeus said, sotto voce. He'd laid Lan on the ground, and covered her with his blood-soaked jacket.

"I think one of these is quite enough." Thuan sighed. He shifted, slowly and ponderously, from dragon to human. It took everything he had: he stood up, swaying, on two legs that suddenly wobbled and betrayed him.

Someone caught him — Asmodeus, the heat of his Fallen magic trembling around Thuan's body. He held Thuan, wordlessly, until the shaking subsided.

"I — I think I can stand up now," Thuan said.

Asmodeus glared at him, but let go. Thuan tried to stand — wobbled, saw the way Asmodeus's muscles tensed again, ready to catch him — and managed to walk towards the nearest pillar and hold on for dear life until the world stopped swaying.

"Take off your clothes," he said, to Asmodeus, who was still watching him.

A raised eyebrow. "How *very* risqué."

Thuan flushed. Asmodeus laughed.

"Not here, somewhere quiet."

"As you wish." Another deeply ironic smile. "But you're coming with me." It was very much an order. Or a threat. Or both.

"I'll keep an eye on the children," Quang Thu said, from her place by the pillar.

Thuan hesitated. But they weren't going that far, and it wasn't like the shrine was huge. "Can you help with the wounds?"

"Not my expertise," Quang Thu said. She looked exhausted, with deep circles under her eyes. Her dragon antlers were drooping, like a kelp without nutrient, and her entire skin was dotted with lustreless scales.

"All right. Take a look at Lan, please?"

Quang Thu nodded.

Inside the shrine, it was dark. The main and only room started as something orderly like in the citadel — wooden screens with exquisite carvings separating the space into smaller rooms where people could worship separately, all broken, all empty — but then it flared out, straight into a cave within the cliff, and the screens disappeared. In that wider, single space, Thuan's eyes made out a statue — an immortal that looked vaguely familar, maybe one of the coral ones? She'd been carrying a basket but now only had the handle, and algae pockmarked the face and the undone hair spilling out from the topknot. Thuan mouthed a silent apology to her, though the *khi*-currents of water didn't move or give any other sign of her presence. There was no magic here, not the way there had been in the Anemone Immortal's shrine. They went deeper into the shrine, behind the statue. It was all cave now, rock beneath their feet and scatterings of dead coral on the ceiling above them. "Here," Thuan said, pointing to a slight depression in the wall.

"Far enough from her?" Asmodeus said. He looked at the statue and then back at Thuan. "We *are* going to strip naked, and I imagine most of your spirits don't approve of random exhibitionism."

"Mmmph." Thuan sighed. "No, but I want to keep an eye on the children, and if we go too deep I won't be able to do that. And thank you. For asking."

Asmodeus shrugged. "You always give up too easily. I'm here to make sure you don't."

Thuan felt his heart flutter in his chest, wobbly and fragile. "Sometimes I could kiss you."

"Only sometimes?" Asmodeus's smile was broad, sharp-toothed.

"When you're not being an utter irritation." He sighed. "Now do what I asked earlier. Take off your clothes so we can look at your wounds. Because don't think I didn't notice how unsteady on your feet you were."

"Only if you do the same."

They stripped in silence, watching each other.

"See?" Asmodeus said. "No wounds."

At least, none that Thuan could see. Asmodeus's chest moved up and down with each breath, and his pale skin was lambent with Fallen magic, swirling as if trapped within him. The scar on his left side — an old, healed thing — rippled with each breath. He could almost *see* Asmodeus's heartbeat, imagine it, steady and strong under his fingers.

Asmodeus stretched his right hand — he'd dropped his gloves — and stared at it for a while.

"What's wrong?" Thuan asked.

"You assume something is wrong."

"Mmm." Thuan watched him for a while. "You're

shaking, aren't you." A minute tremor that most people wouldn't have seen, but Thuan wasn't most people.

"Nothing I can do for that at the moment. Now you," he said, before Thuan had a chance to say something sharp and wounding about ghosts and anchors to ghosts, "don't look fine."

"Is it a competition?"

Asmodeus moved. One moment he was in front of Thuan; the next he stood behind him, bergamot and orange blossom trembling at Thuan's back, his presence tangible and steadying. His hand came up, taking off all the hairpins in Thuan's hair. They clinked as they fell to the floor, one by one. And then Asmodeus's hand was running through his hair, gently untangling strands of it, his fingers dancing gently on Thuan's scalp, a slow and steady touch, a tingling, tightening pleasure. "At least that's healing. It doesn't look burnt anymore. I'm sorry I had to do that," he said. He continued running his hand through Thuan's hair, softly and gently. Thuan leant into the touch, aching with need. "Your hand?"

Thuan sighed. "I'm not sure." He unclenched the hand he had deliberately not been using when taking off his clothes. It looked horrible: the wound still bisected it, and the bone still glistened.

Asmodeus's hand was still running through his hair, steadying him.

"You're distracting me, aren't you."

"Think of it as... emotional comfort."

"Not really what I associate with you," Thuan managed.

"I'm a fast learner. You looked like you were about to collapse."

"We both are, aren't we. About to collapse." It was a sobering feeling to voice aloud, though Thuan had a suspicion Asmodeus was finding it harder to admit than him. And they couldn't afford to collapse, not now. "The children—"

"Leave the children out of this for a minute. Your hand."

Thuan sighed. "I don't know why it's not healing. It's not the paper charms: the other one seems fine." He unfolded that, took a look at it. "Can you stop with the hair for a minute? I'm finding it hard to focus."

Asmodeus's hand stopped. Thuan felt he'd just lost something precious. He wanted to lean back into the touch, to kiss his husband — to do ten thousand things that they didn't have the leisure for. "You're good with wounds. Given the sheer number you've inflicted on other people. Can you take a look at it after we put our clothes back on?"

"I'm glad to have useful skills." Asmodeus's voice was deadpan. "Hang on." He went back to his clothes, quickly put them back on.

By the time he came back — bloodied shirt half-open because he was just that kind of bastard — Thuan was trying to work out the difference between his hands. "The children?"

"Still outside. Sounds like Ai Nhi is trying to teach Camille how to build a miniature dragon with pieces of rubble and coral."

"Is she using magic?" Thuan couldn't envision the smashed-up rocks and fragments of coral amounting to anything. And Ai Nhi's control on the *khi*-currents had improved, but not *that* much.

"No, just her imagination and Camille's imagination." Asmodeus stared at Thuan's hand for a while. "Show me your other one?"

Fallen magic trembled in the air. Asmodeus touched each of Thuan's fingers in turn, carefully hovering above the wound — Thuan sucked in air, bracing himself for pain, but he barely felt Asmodeus's touch, the flare of Fallen magic — and then *something*, he wasn't sure what, changed, and the pain flared up like a spike driven through his hand, all his fingers spasming at the same time, and he screamed and screamed and screamed until his throat felt flayed.

Asmodeus didn't let go. His fingers remained on Thuan's hand — moving slowly and gently and inexorably — while his other arm wrapped around Thuan's body, holding him close. "Done," he said after what felt like an eternity in some court of Hell, and withdrew, but he remained holding Thuan, whispering "sshhh" over and over until the pain went from unbearable to red-hot, and slowly faded.

"That's... not... good," Thuan said. He was still shaking. "I hope you got a good look at it, because I'm not doing it again."

"Don't think you could bear it again," Asmodeus said.

It was curt, annoyed.

"So?"

"Mmm. Some kind of magic is holding it open."

"So poison. Magical. Anything familiar?"

"Mmm. I think not." Asmodeus hated poison. He thought it was too unpredictable, cowardly, and point-less — what was the point of not seeing one's enemies stabbed? But that also meant he'd extensively studied how *not* to get poisoned. "Not Fallen, and not alchemical either. Something dragon-ish. We need to find whoever sent those paper things and... persuade them to explain."

With a very sharp object, no doubt. "It would work if we had any idea who they are, and at the moment we don't. Is it spreading?" Thuan tried to keep his voice steady.

"Not that I can see."

Good. That was one fewer thing to worry about. Though the pain was excruciating even when Asmodeus wasn't touching him. Thuan exhaled, trying to keep it at bay — found Asmodeus's hands on his shoulders, gently steadying him. "Asmodeus—"

"Ssh, dragon prince. I can see how much it hurts. Even now."

"I—" Thuan opened his mouth to say he could bear it, changed his mind. "I could do without the pain. And why this hand?"

"I don't know, but you only have the magic on this one."

Thuan was staring at the wound, at the way the *khi*-currents bent around Asmodeus's Fallen magic. "Oh.

Wait." He called light, watching it shimmer and pool in the hollow of his wounded hand. There was something there where no magic went, faint black squiggles like some secret handwriting.

No, not secret.

"It's Chinese," Thuan said.

"Court language?" Asmodeus asked.

"Yeah. I think—" It looked like some line from a poem, or a court memorial, with flowery, rhythmic language. "*The anemone's blood shrivels under the coldest of moons...*" A spell. "I think it's ink from the charms. It got into this wound, but not the other one. For some reason. Maybe because it's larger."

"Are you really expecting this to be logical?"

"It'd be nice if it was," Thuan said. He looked at his hand again. Not healing. "Reassuring." He tore off his sleeve, started wrapping it around the wound, binding it as tightly as he could.

"Those who set these charms loose surely have an idea of how to heal it. And we'll find them."

Visiting that kind of bloody retribution comforted Asmodeus — it didn't really do anything for Thuan. But then again... it wasn't Thuan Asmodeus was trying to reassure, at the moment. "I'll be fine," Thuan said.

"Oh, dragon prince. You're such a terrible liar."

Thuan did what *he* found comforting: trying to find something that made sense. "Anemone. Like the Anemone Immortal. Maybe Thai Ha didn't die in such a random, isolated place."

"The Anemone Immortal?"

"It's that shrine's name. Hong Chi told me."

A raised eyebrow — usually he'd be annoyed, but now it was almost comforting. "What now?"

The proper thing — in accordance with rituals and his upraising — would have been to get palace help. Notify his grandmother or an eunuch, and get them to look at the problem. Except that — "Those charms aren't chasing us."

"Mm." Asmodeus looked thoughtful.

"It's probably because they lost us, and because we're too far away from the city.

Which means getting back into the palace is going to be a little hard. We risk being swarmed as soon as we get there."

"The palace. You want to go back and throw ourselves on the mercy and skills of the imperial court? Both of which are distinctly lacking, as I recall."

Thuan sighed. "It'd be the right thing to do."

"Do you think that? Truly?" Asmodeus made a face halfway between fondness and exasperation. Of course he disapproved of anyone he couldn't trust looking into their business. But he still asked Thuan, because it mattered.

Thuan considered. It was still hard to trust his gut feelings after a lifetime of being told he was wrong, or a disappointment, or both. But the children's safety was at stake. "They have more resources than we do. We could try sending a message." Somehow.

"Through the *khi*-currents?"

"No," Thuan said. "I can't do that, unless Fallen magic can. It has to have a physical support. A piece of paper."

"Fallen magic can't, no. Not here in the dragon kingdom. Mmm." Asmodeus didn't look wildly enthusiastic, and that was the understatement of the century. "That seems like a lot of hassle for not a lot of gain."

"I guess the real question is why they're chasing us. To silence the g — Lan? But why not do that as soon as we picked Lan up?"

"I imagine it took time for news of who we'd picked up to make their way to whoever has a guilty conscience."

"I'm not sure they've got a guilty conscience so much as a fear of being caught."

"Good. Fear will prevent them from making smart decisions."

"Let's go talk to Quang Thu," Thuan said. "After you get dressed properly. And probably after we put the children to bed."

Asmodeus shrugged, but he closed the buttons on his shirt.

They emerged into late evening. The sun, as it always did in the dragon kingdom, had set without so much as a glimmer of pink or purple: the sky was dark, and the stars impossibly small and far away, the constellations so different from the ones above Paris.

Quang Thu had got the children settled down on some of the rubble in the courtyard. They were nibbling on rice cakes, which appeared to be Ai Nhi's emergency stash. Ai Nhi jumped up in a cloud of dust when she saw them.

"Unka Thuan! Unka Asmo! Are you all right?"

Thuan contemplated lying to her. It was really, really tempting, but nothing good ever came of lying to children. "Not right now, but your uncle and I are taking care of it."

Asmodeus muttered something that sounded like "with extreme prejudice". Thuan ignored him.

"Where are the paper things?" Camille asked.

"An *excellent* question," Asmodeus said, "Unka Thuan and I think they can't come here."

"They can't," Quang Thu said. "The exorcist needs to be nearby. And I'm shielding us, at least for the night."

"Thank you," Thuan said.

"Good," Asmodeus said, curtly. He sat on one of the rocks by Ai Nhi's side, his body posture clearly signifying he wasn't providing cuddles — something he only grudgingly gave anyway. Camille threw him a look, and went into Thuan's arms instead, burrowing into his chest. He tried not to wince when she hit the bandaged hand, but Camille saw it anyway.

"You hurt your hand, Unka," she said. "I'll kiss it better."

Awww. It didn't really help with the healing, but it did make him feel better.

"Do you want a rice cake?" Ai Nhi said to Asmodeus. "It's good for healing."

Asmodeus looked grudgingly impresssed. "How did you hide these?"

Ai Nhi waved. "In my sleeves right next to the knife!"

Asmodeus held out his hand. "Fair. I could use some food. Thank you."

Ai Nhi beamed. "Here, Unka Asmo!"

Thuan couldn't help smiling as he took half a rice cake. "A good sense of priorities."

Asmodeus caught Quang Thu's gaze — held it for a while. His hand drew a symbol — the Southern character for "Orchid" — Lan in Viet. His gaze went, quick and fast, to Ai Nhi and Camille. The message was clear: as much as could be told in front of the children.

Thuan sighed. "Asmodeus, they can hear whatever Quang Thu has to say."

"They're eight and five."

"Yes," Thuan said. "They've also seen you fight guards and me being hurt by paper charms. Not to mention a dead body and a ghost."

Asmodeus's gaze narrowed. He was about to start a fight on the ghost — he thought Lan was a child, heedless of the fact maintaining her in the mortal world was draining him, or the fact one couldn't trust ghosts to be kind — but then he checked himself with an obvious effort. Which meant he was really exhausted, or it'd have been smoother.

Thuan tried not to worry. Unfortunately, 'worry' was his default state of being. "Anyway," he said, "you can't shelter them. Not from *this*. It'll just be scarier."

A pause. Asmodeus cocked his head, watching the children. The lenses of his glasses glinted in the light. "You have a point," he said, grudgingly. "Quang Thu?"

Quang Thu looked impressed — an expression Thuan was all too used to, except that it usually was when looking at Asmodeus. This time it seemed to be reserved for Thuan, which was a deuced odd and uncomfortable feeling. Thuan was mostly used to people being disappointed in him — including Asmodeus over this whole ghost business, a thought that still annoyed and unsettled him. "I can't wake Lan up," Quang Thu said, finally. "There's nothing wrong with her, but she's just not conscious."

Thuan considered how to phrase the next question to prevent his husband from being upset — which he wouldn't, per se, *say* — he would just become terribly unpleasant. "Is it because we're too far away from her body?"

"No," Quang Thu said. "The anchor is enough, with ghosts like her. And she's fed recently."

On Asmodeus. Who looked weary and stressed, and most definitely unlikely to admit those facts to anyone. He smiled. "Good enough?" he asked Thuan.

Of course he knew the question Thuan hadn't asked, which was how weak he was.

Thuan sighed, and deflected. "All right," he said. "We'll take a look after bedtime and see how we can help her." It might be poison from the charms, but he didn't want the conversation to head that way, because he'd have to tell the children a little more than he felt comfortable with.

"No bedtime!" Camille said, wailing.

"Oh yes," Thuan said, firmly. "Being away from the palace isn't an excuse, child." He saw, from the corner of his eye, that Asmodeus had cleared away a space with two makeshift beds, one on each step of the temple entrance.

Ai Nhi looked crestfallen. "That's very unfair," she said, dragon antlers flickering into existence around her face. "You get to have all the adult fun."

Adult fun — in this specific case, figuring out what was wrong with a ghost — was really overrated. "Bed. Now," Thuan said. "Now am I in charge of storytelling, or is it Unka Asmo?"

It took more time than usual to settle the children. They weren't in their usual beds — twice removed from the safety of House Hawthorn — they'd been chased and seen their parental figures hurt, and to say they were wired was a huge understatement. Thuan ended up curling up with Ai Nhi, running through grounding exercises with her and using just a touch of *khi*-water to soothe her.

He walked down the steps and back to their improvised dinner site to find Asmodeus already kneeling by Lan's side. Quang Thu was sitting on the floor between patches of whitened coral, writing something on what looked like a personal journal with a fountain pen — an oddity in the dragon kingdom where paintbrushes were more common.

"Camille?" Thuan asked.

"She's fine," Asmodeus said. "Fell asleep like a log."

"Ai Nhi was really scared of the charms."

A shrug, from Asmodeus. "I told Camille I'd stab

whoever had sent them."

"That's cheating."

A smile — and a finger, running on his lips until Thuan ached for more. The air roiled with Fallen magic, and with a faint smell of bergamot and citrus. "Not my fault if you're squeamish, dragon prince."

Mostly it was that Thuan wouldn't sound convincing even if he did say it, and they both knew it. Asmodeus still had his finger on Thuan's lips. Thuan gave in, and bent to kiss Asmodeus — who kissed him back, the feel of his warm lips on Thuan's spreading a tight, pleasant feeling of desire into Thuan's entire body. "What do you have?"

"Not sure. Quang Thu thinks Lan is unconscious because of the effort of downing all those charms in the courtyard. When she screamed." He *was* worried. Asmodeus's magic trembled on Lan's shape, lighting up the ghost's slight form. He frowned. "We've seen this before, haven't we."

"Yes," Thuan — who had the better eye for detail — called up the *khi*-currents, flooding Lan with magic. "Look," he said.

On Lan's skin were the same faint squiggles as on Thuan's hand, except — "The handwriting is different," Thuan said.

Asmodeus raised an eyebrow. "How can you tell?"

"He's right," Quang Thu said.

Thuan hadn't seen her come. Her notebook was still in her hand; the diffuse night light made her seem phantasmagorical, almost like a ghost herself. She ran a hand over her shaved head, frowning.

"It's Southern characters. *A handful of anemones by the side of the road, beasts on robes and flags fluttering in the breeze...*"

"It sounds like a prayer," Thuan said.

"It is one." Quang Thu's voice was curt. "The rhythm is very distinctive."

"To the Anemone Immortal? So it *is* connected to the shrine," Thuan said. He looked at his hand again. If he didn't think about it too much, it barely hurt. And he knew *exactly* the kind of frown Asmodeus would have if he ever said that aloud. "And the charms don't like the Anemone Immortal. How has this got anything to do with Lan? Or with Thai Ha's murder?"

"Thai Ha *was* going to worship the Immortal, wasn't she?" Asmodeus made a gesture, and the light of his magic vanished. He sat back, brushing a stray length of hair from Lan's face — way too ramrod and stiff as opposed to his usual fluid movements. He was in pain again.

"Yes, but that's not the reason she was—" Thuan opened his mouth, closed it. What was it his tutors had said? Always be ready to reassess a given situation. "You thought she'd gotten killed because of the promotion," he said to Quang Thu.

"It made sense." Quang Thu waved the piece of paper again — the one on which she'd written the names of every one of their suspects. Not that they'd had time, in all the confusion, to actually do anything about the murder. "And someone was sending the charms to silence Lan as a witness."

Thuan stared at Lan again — small and unconscious, utterly unmoving, her skin yellowed like old parchment, her lips the faded, brownish red of meat turning spoiled. He spread the weave of his *khi*-currents over her whole body. The writing was all over her skin — no, not just all over her skin, it had sunk deep into her, as if her whole being were made of tightly packed letters. "It made sense," he said slowly, softly. "But that doesn't explain why the charms speak of anemones. Or the writing on Lan."

"A side effect of the magic?" Asmodeus said.

"Hmmm." Thuan said. He was starting to suspect the Anemone Immortal was central to all of this, and they needed more information. "You're going to hate this," he said to Asmodeus.

"Try me."

"We need to find a way to get into the Ministry of Justice's archives."

"Sneaking into the palace while being chased by extremely persistent paper charms?" Asmodeus snorted. "Did you just pick the one thing we both are abysmal at and add extra difficulty to it?"

Thuan said, "I was thinking Quang Thu could do it."

"Perhaps, assuming the charms are just going after Lan," Quang Thu said. "Why?"

"I want to know if there have been other murders in that shrine, particularly of officials."

"You have an idea?"

"Mmm. More like a theory," Thuan said. He moved his

hand to dismiss the weave of *khi*-currents, winced when the open wound on his hand hurt. "I think it is linked to the shrine, but I'm not sure why yet. "

"Hmm. Fair," Quang Thu said. "I'll have a look tomorrow. I also have an idea."

"Do tell," Thuan said.

"About the charms," Quang Thu said. She held up one.

"Whoa, careful." Thuan took a step away from her.

"It's inert." Quang Thu said. She waved it in the air. It was whole, but the writing on it was singed. "It's one that was in your mane. Asmodeus singed it with Fallen magic." She pointed to the writing, which was now illegible black, as if the ink had run under a downpour. "His magic cut the link to the exorcist. That's why it's inert."

"I'm not sure—" Thuan said.

Quang Thu frowned. "I think I could probably rewrite the script on them."

"You can make your own paper charms, surely?" Thuan asked. He wasn't very well versed in exorcisms — he'd seldom had to deal with them.

"I could. But these came from somewhere. I think we could send them back to where they came from with very little effort. Like an elastic. They remember where they came from, and it's a simpler suggestion than to go looking for someone with charms. Even if we did know who we were looking for."

Which, at the moment, they didn't. "How many do you have?"

"Not many," Quang Thu's face was inexpressive. "So

far."

She had a point. It was too much to hope that the exorcist was going to stop sending charms after them. "Fair. Can you look into it?"

Next to them, Asmodeus rose, with a barely perceptible grimace. He was carrying Lan. Lan's mouth was open, revealing sharp teeth, blood glimmering on them — her skin the colour of broken porcelain, shimmering and sheening. Her arms dangled from Asmodeus's grip. Where they brushed the fabric of Asmodeus's swallowtail suit, the sharp fingertips slashed into the cloth. Asmodeus merely gathered her closer, whispering "ssh", as if she were a frightened child. As if she didn't look like something straight out of nightmares, something that would pull out his entrails and eat them when the hunger got too much. Something that was already eating him alive to exist.

"What are you doing?" Thuan asked, though he already knew.

"Making sure she sleeps somewhere safe," Asmodeus said. "She needs to feel secure if she wakes up."

She was not a child. She would never be a child. Thuan forced himself to breathe. "Asmodeus, I've already told you—"

"Precisely." Asmodeus's voice was curt. "You already told me. I'm not interested in your scared and squeamish justifications for why we shouldn't help the weak. Or in having this conversation at all, dragon prince."

He was not squeamish, not on this! "She's not weak!"

Thuan said, but Asmodeus was already gone inside, with Lan in his arms.

Quang Thu had gone back to sitting back against her pillar. She was pointedly not looking at Thuan. He felt obscurely embarrassed, as if she'd witnessed some kind of personal failure from him. And perhaps she had — Asmodeus was so angry at Thuan. He said, finally, "We're not like this, usually."

Quang Thu said nothing for a while. Then she set aside her notebook. "Quarrelling in a crisis? You'd hardly be the first couple to do so."

"He—" Thuan said. "He just thinks of her as a normal child."

"And you don't." It was said in a carefully neutral tone.

Thuan felt obscurely ashamed. Or angry. He wasn't sure anymore. "I — look. She had a horrible death. And not, I would guess, the best of afterlives." She should have gone through the courts of hell, been swept up in another reincarnation. Given another chance at a life where people wouldn't fail her.

"No," Quang Thu said.

Thuan could hear Asmodeus's voice, slow and grave — at first he thought it was a children's tale, but then he realised it had the lilt and cadence of a lullaby. "I've never heard him sing," he said. Not even at Catholic mass, which Asmodeus attended with great seriousness and didn't otherwise take part in — he'd said once that he was under no illusion about what God thought of him, and there was no point in any further interactions. Like

63

all Fallen angels, Asmodeus didn't remember anything from his life in Heaven, including the offence that had seen him cast down. Thuan suspected he'd be proud of it rather than repentant: he had embraced his Fall without shame or regret. And yet, he still came to mass. Hoping for something? Trying to confront God?

"And you're jealous he's giving her what you've never seen him give you. Or the children you're raising," Quang Thu said.

"No!" Thuan said. Whatever his own faults, jealousy was singularly lacking. He sighed. "Look, I know why he's doing it. He's always had a weak spot for the lost and broken, and he feels no one is treating her like they should." And if there was anything Asmodeus was good at besides stabbing, it was stepping up when no one did, or when he thought no one did.

"And are they?" Quang Thu's gaze was piercing.

"She's a *ghost*," Thuan said. "Tell me what happens when she gets hungry."

"Now? Or before I anchored her?"

Thuan just stared at her.

Quang Thu shrugged. "If she gets hungry she'll feed on blood and attack passers-by to get the blood. And now — she'll just feed on your husband. Is that why you asked about the murders in the shrine?" Her eyes were hard.

"No!" Thuan forced himself to take a deep breath. "The shrine is deserted. She'll have been going out and attacking passers-by, not killing them there." And there had been no bones other than Lan's. "You can't seriously tell me you're defending a ghost."

"The boundary between life and death isn't as absolute as you seem to think it is," Quang Thu said. "You're right, though. Nothing but Asmodeus's life sustains her in this world, and she's requiring most of it to not fade."

"You tied him to *this*?"

A silence. Quang Thu was watching him with a smile that was eerily reminiscent of Asmodeus. "He volunteered. And all he has to is ask me to end it, and I will."

Thuan thought of Asmodeus three years ago in the grove at House Hawthorn, kneeling pale-faced and almost voiceless on the ground — giving everything he had in order to preserve the House rather than admit defeat, or the risk to his own life. "You know he won't—" Thuan started, and then stopped. Asmodeus would rather die than fail Lan. That was the gist of it, wasn't it, the fear he was turning into anger at Quang Thu. "I'm sorry. You're not the one I'm angry at."

Quang Thu made an expansive gesture with her sleeves.

"What will happen to Lan?" Thuan asked. "After it... ends." He kept his voice calm. It took an effort.

"She'll move on," Quang Thu said. "Or she'll need to be exorcised, if she doesn't."

"Because of what she needs." Because she'd keep drinking blood and life, and killing others. Because it was her nature.

"She needs life," Quang Thu said. "And she doesn't have it, not anymore."

A sound, nearby: Asmodeus, moving back into the light, his arms empty. He picked a place by a pillar, and sat against it, stiff — closing his eyes for a bare moment, as if he were going to doze off, before sitting bolt upright once more. Then he got out a book — Thuan knew it was in his inner jacket pocket, but he hardly saw Asmodeus move — and started reading it, heedless of the dark. The lenses of his glasses glinted in the little light there was.

No, Lan didn't have life anymore. Trouble was, she had Asmodeus's life, and Thuan didn't really know how to convince his husband it was a terrible, terrible idea to so casually give that away.

In the early morning, Thuan waited until Quang Thu had left for the palace and the imperial archives before starting a conversation with Asmodeus. The children were still asleep. Asmodeus was sitting on a rock with barnacles, his gloves by his side, eating a soggy leftover oil-fried pastry. Thuan had a vague suspicion he'd grabbed it from the meal he'd never got to finish before the charms attacked.

"I want to go into the capital," Thuan said.

Asmodeus looked up from his pastry, a fraction less gracious and elegant than he usually was. "Why?"

"I... know someone," Thuan said. "Well, I slept with her half a century ago but that's not why I want to see her."

"I assume not. Though if you would like to have sex to

relieve the tension I'm happy to oblige." Asmodeus's lips curled up in the ghost of a smile. They'd both had a score of prior relationships, and neither of them was really the jealous type.

"With the children nearby?" Thuan realised as soon as he'd said it what Asmodeus's answer would be.

"There are ways." A hint of magic seized Thuan's limbs and froze them for a bare moment — followed by a gentle caress on his lips, slow but insistent — and another set of them climbing up his spine.

"Asmodeus..."

Asmodeus smiled, and it was wide and wicked — and for a moment, a bare moment, everything was well, and they weren't on the run with the issue of Lan between them. As if he were lying back on the bed at Hawthorn, Asmodeus' magic holding him still while his touch set Thuan afire.

He wanted it, so badly. Not just the sex, but the illusion that nothing and no one could touch what they had. "I want to, but we really can't."

Asmodeus kept up the magic for a fraction of a second more — and Thuan was hard, breathing through a haze of desire — and then the magic... didn't die so much as reluctantly fade. "Shall we say another time?"

"Not yet." Thuan kissed Asmodeus, a desperately needed outlet for his frustration. "Just this." Heaven, just this please, this arcing, roiling storm of need finding some closure.

Asmodeus kissed him back. It was slow and forceful,

and Thuan felt like he was swallowing live, molten honey, a jolt that went straight through his chest — while being held in an unbreakable embrace, with the utter certainty that Asmodeus wouldn't falter or let go.

"Dragon prince."

They held on to each other for a while more, Thuan breathing Asmodeus's trembling heat — trying not to notice how it was weaker and less steady than the force of nature he usually seemed like.

"Anyway, I want to talk to my friend. She graduated first in the metropolitan exams about a century or so ago, and she specialises in healing spells. She left the Academy of the Forest of Brushes because she didn't really like the politics, and now she's an apothecary in the biggest dispensary. If anyone can fix the wounds of the charms, it's probably her."

"We could ask the wielder of the charms."

"And face them while weak? I really don't like the idea, and I don't think you like it more than I do."

"Fair." Asmodeus pondered, for a while. "You go, then. I'll keep an eye on the children."

Oh. He hadn't thought it through, but that would be a disaster. "That's not a good solution," Thuan said, reflexively.

Asmodeus shrugged. "Are you suggesting we take the children into town?"

"No!" Thuan said, horrified. They were too distinctive, and even more so as a group.

"Then that's the setup that makes the most sense. Go

make your inquiries in town, try not to stand out, and come back."

Thuan opened his mouth, closed it.

"Don't trust me to babysit?" Asmodeus's voice was light and ironic.

I don't trust you to stay alive, Thuan wanted to say, but the words remained stuck in his throat. "Did you sleep at all?"

"Very poorly." Asmodeus stared at him as if daring to make a further commentary.

Words came welling out of Thuan like blood from a wound. "She'll be the death of you, and you know it."

"Another attempt to rehash a fruitless argument?" Asmodeus finished eating his pastry, brushed crumbs off his hands. "I've already told you I'm not interested."

"And am I just expected to sit still and silent until you drive yourself past what you can bear?"

"You'll notice I'm not making decisions for you, as evidenced by the fact I haven't even dissuaded you from your doomed and risky plan to enter the capital unnoticed," Asmodeus said. "Don't make them for me, dragon prince."

"It's not a doomed plan!"

"Is it?" Asmodeus raised an eyebrow. "Your clothes and your bearing stink of privilege. You're a fundamentally honest and decent person." He said it like it was a personal flaw. "You lie about as well as a toddler caught red-handed in the biscuit box, and I've handled my share of these. I give you about a quarter of a bi hour, maximum, before the alert is raised everywhere over town."

That stung. Asmodeus was dressing him down like a child, each sentence a knife slid between Thuan's ribs — and it was the contemptuous annoyance that hurt the most. "You think I'm incompetent."

"No," Asmodeus said. "Naive."

And that didn't hurt less. "From the one who tied his own life to a ghost and won't let go? You're *reckless*!"

"You just don't understand what duty is about."

"I understand she's dead! She'll kill people to survive! How can you possibly think that's an acceptable state of affairs?"

Asmodeus's face went very still. "Acceptable." His eyes were hard, the anger and contempt withering. "Acceptable. You understand nothing, don't you. About who I am, what I do."

How could he — ? "I understand you blame me for putting myself in harm's way but aren't capable of applying your advice to yourself!"

Asmodeus's eyes blazed. His whole body tensed. His mouth opened on something — Thuan should have cared, should have been afraid of the verbal flaying, but he was so angry — how dare he give lessons he couldn't even be bothered to follow? How dare he be so condescending, so fundamentally *unpleasant*?

"Unka Thuan? Unka Asmo?"

Asmodeus turned, whiplash-fast — Thuan a fraction of a moment later. It was Ai Nhi, rubbing her eyes and standing by an algae-encrusted pillar. "Why are you fighting?"

"We're not—" Thuan opened his mouth, closed it. No, lying was a terrible idea. "Adult things. Come here."

Ai Nhi looked from him to Asmodeus — whose face was now composed, neutral and distant, his whole body language relaxed. He'd always been more poker-faced than Thuan.

"I hate it when you fight," Ai Nhi said, but walked up to Thuan and buried her face against his chest for a hug. Thuan tried to will away the tension in his entire body. Ai Nhi moved to stand closer to Asmodeus — who gently and uncharacteristically tussled her hair, hands catching, briefly, the ghostly antlers of her dragon shape — and, after some hesitation, drew him close to her for an even briefer hug. Ai Nhi looked from him to Thuan — obviously wondering if she could draw both of them together — and must have decided it wasn't worth trying. "Are you going to fix it?"

"If it can be fixed." Asmodeus's voice was distant. "In the meantime, your unka needs to go check something in town, I believe—" that was a dismissal if Thuan ever heard one — "so we're all going to stay here until he does."

"Oh." Ai Nhi's face brightened. "Does that mean you'll tell us ghost stories?" Asmodeus's idea of ghost stories were the scary and bloody ones, which Ai Nhi absolutely loved.

Asmodeus's face relaxed a fraction. "Maybe," he said. "Show me that knife in your sleeves again, first. I want to teach you a few things." And stared at Thuan as if daring him to contradict what he was doing.

Thuan was angry and upset, but not devoid of practical sense. "Show him," he said to Ai Nhi. "There are enough things after us. You need to be able to defend yourself."

"Attack being the best defence," Asmodeus said. Ai Nhi held out the knife, and he withdrew one of his own from his jacket pocket, angling it to catch the light. "Here. Shift your grip. It's too tense. You want that knife back after you sink it into someone's flesh, and that won't happen if you lack control of where you stab."

Asmodeus was very clearly not looking at Thuan. Not that Thuan felt like doing much of anything except yelling at him for lacking common sense and a self-preservation instinct. "I'll go," he said, and left without looking back.

Are you going to fix it?

If it can be fixed.

They'd had much worse fights than this one. They'd weathered them — talked to each other or tried to. Hells, they'd first met when Asmodeus tried to kill Thuan, and Thuan had run him through with a sword before he could get around to it. But something about this one felt raw and hurtful — as if it was splitting open their relationship on its weakest points.

Are you going to fix it?

He hoped they could. Somehow.

Despite Asmodeus's dire warnings, Thuan slipped into the capital with scarcely a second glance from the guards. These past years, when coming back to the imperial citadel, he'd followed his grandmother's advice of always having an escape strategy, and had pulled rank in the Ministry of Personnel to get a pass made out to a minor clerk of the Bureau of Worship and Sacrifices: a job that required checking supplies within the city and ancestral temples outside of it, and a sufficiently obscure one that no one would pay particular heed to him.

His dress — the one with the yellow dragon that marked his status as an imperial prince — was a little more troublesome. He took some time summoning *khi*-water and doing the best he could to alter its patterns, so that it read generically wealthy but not like imperial blood. Thank Heaven he was no longer in the contention for the succession of Second Aunt, or he'd have had a much larger dragon embroidery to disguise.

It was a busy morning in the city: sellers of street food; dragons, crabs, and other sea spirits on their way to the market, the shops, the restaurants and their appointments. Palanquin bearers regularly attempted to clear their way through the din, and the air was saturated with the smell of food — almost enough to cover the ever-present one of decay. Thuan stopped by a pillar whose upper part was all graceful paintings of the Eight Immortals, and whose lower part was eaten away by algae and mould, the rock faces indistinguishable.

The dispensary was full, and the apothecary at the front of the shop unpleasant and rude, taking Thuan's personal seal with a sniff and a shake of her dragon antlers. Thuan gazed back at her, levelly, and settled down to wait: it wasn't long at all before she came back, and showed him into a room clearly meant for examinations, with spare and utilitarian furniture, a saturation of *khi*-currents, and nothing in there but a teapot and a single cup of tea.

Thuan picked it up, sipped it. It was a grassy green tea that smelled of ripe flowers and apricots, and left a dry, pleasant mouthfeel, a far distance from the tea in Hawthorn — acrid and black, and which Asmodeus had a tendency to drink overbrewed because he liked the acridity and tea was low on his list of priorities.

"Well, that's a surprise," a voice said.

Thuan looked up from the tea. Diem Chau stood in the doorway. She was wearing the indigo robes of an apothecary, with a profusion of golden hairpins in her topknot — and long flowing hair falling down her back, the white spots of her orca shape shimmering beneath the ceruse covering her face. She was pristine and sharp, as elegant as always — wearing makeup and ornaments like finely-honed weapons. He breathed in, and abruptly he was fifty years younger, breathing in water lilies as he powdered them to make a medicine her dispensary needed, and her hands covered his, her lips ghosting the back of his nape — what he wouldn't have given to be back then, in simpler times.

He sighed, struggling to compose himself. She was looking at him with a question on her lips: he forestalled her. "Hello, lil'sis," Thuan said. "I need some help."

"So I gather." Diem Chau laughed. "Didn't think you'd

be dropping by the dispensary if you didn't."

"I can give you the standard treatment if you'd rather," Thuan said. "Though it'd have to be at a restaurant where they don't know me." They'd remained good friends after they'd broken up, and prior to Thuan's departure from the dragon kingdom to marry Asmodeus. Once or twice a month they'd have a long dinner and a walk through the streets, remaking the world several times over. Now that he was in Hawthorn, he seldom saw her, but they wrote to each other. "I can't exactly afford to be recognised right now."

"Ah. That bad?" Diem Chau came to sit by his side. She smelled of blood and spices, the narrow angles of her face inquisitive. Her skin was dark and glistening. "Who's looking for you?"

"I don't know," Thuan said. "Yet."

"Mmm. The palace has been very silent lately."

"It's not like I make palace news."

"You? No. Your husband, though..."

"Be fair! He's mellowed."

"From terrifying disaster to impolite inconvenience? Yes, but even mellow isn't good enough for the court." Diem Chau snorted. "They want everything in harmony and order. Except perhaps your grandmother."

Thuan's grandmother was a force of nature, an utterly scary old woman and a big proponent of killing everyone who stood in her way. She and Asmodeus had hit it off almost immediately.

"Mmm. How have you been? How's the business

expansion going?" He knew from her last letter that the dispensary — which she now co-owned with two of the other apothecaries — had had a number of high-profile cases that had helped drive customers to it.

"Politics," Diem Chau made a face. "We're talking about opening another branch in the province of Dai Anh. I'm seriously considering moving there."

"That bad?"

Diem Chau's face closed. "When you insist ministers get priority over others for their medication? Or gently discourage us from providing care to people they don't approve of?"

Thuan winced. Nothing surprising, but still. "And your partners?"

"Disinclined to push back. They say things about the importance of good relationships, about how we need the court for our customers, how it serves the greater good of our patients. I hear nothing but cowardice."

Cowardice.

Thuan heard Asmodeus's voice in his head, and he suddenly had the horrible suspicion that Diem Chau and Asmodeus would get along like a house on fire. What this said about his dating preferences he'd rather not think about at the moment.

"Who's doing that? I could help."

"Mmm. You could, but you sound like you've got a lot going on," Diem Chau said. She rubbed his shoulder gently. "Tell you what. I'll send you the names when you're in a better position, and in exchange you tell me what exactly is bothering you, and why you show up at my place of work rather than invite me to tea and dumplings."

"Let's just say this is at the point where I'm tempted to ask my grandmother for help," Thuan said, wryly.

"That bad, huh." Diem Chau produced an extra teacup out of seemingly nowhere — probably the wide sleeves of her embroidered robes — and poured herself another cup of tea. "Why don't you tell me."

When Thuan was done, she was silent for a while. Her gaze was hard. "Ghosts and charms. I see. Show me your wound?"

Thuan had forgotten it was there. Diem Chau undid the bandages that kept it wrapped up. Thuan winced as pain flared up, and then again as magic, merciless, poked and prodded.

"Keep still," Diem Chau said, sternly. Her weavings of *khi*-currents looped around Thuan's hand — water and a touch of wood, tight traceries of power that made Thuan bite his lip. And then a spike of pain that made him want to scream as the characters within the wound shone a deep, vermillion red. Diem Chau held the weaving a moment more, and then dropped it.

"Are you all right?"

"No," Thuan hissed between closed lips. All he wanted was to curl up in a ball, but most definitely not in front of Diem Chau — there were limits to his appetite for embarrassment. "I'll — survive."

Diem Chau had the grace not to say anything. Her loops of *khi*-water sank into Thuan's hand, cool and soothing. "This should help. Magical wounds require magic to fix. And I'm going to give you an unguent. Make sure you put that on, or they're going to scar."

"Great," Thuan said. "Just great. Ghosts, magical wounds, bloodthirsty charms. Just what I needed."

"What you need," Diem Chau said, sternly, "is rest. Several good nights' sleep, and no exertion. Though." She paused.

"I don't like the 'though'," Thuan said. Or the rest of the advice: he felt called out on some obscure sins he didn't even remember having committed. It wasn't like he'd had a choice about being on the run. "Can you tell me about the spell? It's linked to the Anemone Immortal, isn't it?"

"I assume," Diem Chau said.

"You don't know? What is it that's making you unhappy then?"

Diem Chau was silent for a while. "That spell's style is very distinctive. What did you do to incur the enmity of the head of the Exorcist Guild, Thuan?"

"We knew it was an exorcist."

"He's *the* exorcist," Diem Chau said. "Khac Anh. And he's the one behind the paper charms that hurt you, with absolute certainty." She made a face.

Uh. Good news, they had a name and presumably a way of finding who was behind it all. Bad news, Diem Chau looked unusually preoccupied. "You don't like him," Thuan said. "And for more reasons than just his hurting me, I assume."

Diem Chau poured herself another cup of tea, and one for Thuan. Her skin sheened orca-black. "Have some tea," she said.

"Seriously. I'm not a child. I can take the unpleasantness."

"Khac Anh is the kind of man who makes your husband look *nice*," Diem Chau said.

Thuan opened his mouth to protest that Asmodeus had few principles but at least he had very clear ones, and then closed it.

"You were going to protest your husband was nice, weren't you. Are you that besotted with him?"

Currently, Thuan didn't know where he stood. But he did know that anyone who used "nice" and "Asmodeus" in the same sentence was likely to get stabbed by Asmodeus. "You're going to have to define 'not nice'."

"Ruthless. Power hungry. Controlling. Doesn't like to be told no."

That was significantly worse than Asmodeus on so many levels. "I don't suppose you know where he lives."

Diem Chau gestured towards the back of the room. "The Guild is that way, and his private villa that way. All public knowledge. But they're both heavily defended. Are you just planning to let your husband loose on them and see what happens?"

Thuan would have liked to do that, but even his absolute belief in Asmodeus's capacity to hurt people didn't extend to a frontal assault on a fortified place. "I'd like to know why Khac Anh is involved. To dispel a rogue ghost?"

"I'd be very surprised if it's the ghost," Diem Chau said. "Your ghost is under the charge of Quang Thu, and under control. And there are easier targets: the capital is rife with hungry ghosts who've failed to be fed enough. A lot of the tombs don't have their worship maintained, and the paths aren't safe at night. You said you had a theory."

"Yes," Thuan said. "Just not one that involved exorcists. And I'm not sure it's a good one at the moment. I'd rather wait for Quang Thu to come back from the Ministry of Justice."

"You mentioned the Anemone Immortal."

"I think it's linked to her. But how?"

"Mmm. You also said the ghost had other writing on her." Diem Chau finished her tea. "I'd need to have a closer look at her. Lan, you said?"

"Lan," Thuan said, remembering Asmodeus's voice saying her name, and the wounding words they'd exchanged. "Yes. I can't bring her into the city."

"Oh, I wasn't thinking about that." Diem Chau made a gesture, and the teacup went back into her sleeve. "I'll come and have a look. And you can introduce me to your husband."

Thuan opened his mouth. "You do know—"

"Exactly who he is. Absolutely." Diem Chau's smile was bright and cheerful and full of amused curiosity, and Thuan suddenly had the feeling of standing in the way of an oncoming train. "I've been quite looking forward to meeting him."

Quang Thu caught up with them just outside the city gates. She was breathing hard, and some of her monkish clothing was rumpled, as if she'd just been through a clothes-wringer. "Something the matter?" Thuan asked.

"Let's just walk," Quang Thu said. "Away. I had to sneak out of the citadel. No charms, though. I'm starting to suspect—"

"They're tracking Lan," Thuan said, bleakly. "Yes. So did I." As a witness to the crime, to silence her? But why? And why the head of exorcists? "Does the palace know we've vanished?"

"It's not public yet," Quang Thu said. "I think your cousin is keeping a tight wrap on it."

And no wonder. The last few years had been bad, with abysmal harvests and civil unrest, and though the situation was marginally improving with new laws and fewer corrupt officials, everyone was still on edge. The idea that someone might have kidnapped a prince of the realm and his foreigner husband in the middle of the Empress's own citadel would be like tinder to the dry wood of the city's unease.

"She's probably sent her spies to keep an eye out," Thuan said. But it wouldn't occur for spies to look for them in the deserted shrine. At least, not yet. "Oh, this is Diem Chau. She's... a friend."

Diem Chau bowed to Quang Thu, seizing her up. "A magistrate?"

Quang Thu stood still, watching Diem Chau in turn. "You're Diem Chau," she said. "The head apothecary in the Cinnabar Sea Dispensary. I've heard of you in cases." Her tone was respectful.

Diem Chau bowed. "Glad my name gets around. I'm giving Thuan some help with whatever's hunting you around. Sounds like you're in a very large mess."

Thuan said, "Diem Chau knows who's after us."

"Oh?" Quang Thu said.

"Khac Anh," Diem Chau said, curtly.

Quang Thu's face froze. "That's... not an enemy I'd want to make."

"Me neither," Thuan said. And, to Diem Chau, "Are you really sure you want to be helping?"

"How about I'll tell you when I get uncomfortable," Diem Chau said.

They walked down the road to the deserted shrine where Asmodeus and the children were walking. Silt billowed with every one of their steps. Diem Chau was half in orca shape, with a much larger maw and sharp, pointed teeth. Quang Thu said, "You were right about the murders. How did you know?"

"What did you find?"

Quang Thu said, "There have been five over the last hundred years or so. All in the shrine or close to it. I brought copies of the case files if you're interested."

Anything written was like catnip to Thuan, but at

the moment even the thought of curling up with very large piles of written materials didn't spark much joy. He and Asmodeus were barely talking to each other; his husband's life was tied to a ghost, and they now had an unknown and persistent feud with the largest and most powerful exorcist in the city. "I'll settle for the gist of them," he said, and looked away from Diem Chau to not see the pity in her eyes.

"Not much to say. Similar stabbings. People coming to worship the Anemone Immortal for various reasons. Mostly officials praying for a post." Quang Thu frowned. "Remember how the wound that killed Thai Ha was from a thin and pointed blade? Asmodeus thought it was a hairpin."

Diem Chau was nodding, sharply. "You know?" Quang Thu asked.

"A nail," Diem Chau said. "One of the long steel ones that exorcists use to pin down ghosts. Could also be used to hit a real person's pressure points."

Quang Thu gestured to a point on her chest. "Here?" she said.

"That's one of the paralysis ones," Diem Chau said.

"And where Thai Ha was stabbed the first time," Thuan said, sharply.

"Oh, not just Thai Ha. All the previous victims, too." Quang Thu's voice was bleak. They were nearing the sand path leading to the shrine. Soon, Thuan would have to face Asmodeus again. To try and have a conversation about where to take this — any of this — forward, and he just wasn't looking forward to being verbally flayed. Or to wounding Asmodeus as deeply as Asmodeus was wounding him.

"So paralysed and then stabbed to death? Charming," Thuan said.

"There are much, much worse ways to go," Diem Chau said, matter-of-factly, her small sharp teeth shining in her mouth. "Trust me."

"I don't need details," Thuan said. She and Asmodeus were *definitely* going to get on too well.

"You sent me to the Ministry because you had a theory," Quang Thu said. "Does this help?"

It'd better, considering the risks she'd taken. Thuan said, "Yes. I thought it might be the cult being targeted, not just one official and the witness to her murder. But why Khac Anh? Immortals aren't within the purview of exorcists. They're not a threat to the living."

"Ah. His name did come up." Quang Thu started fishing in her ample sleeves for some of the documents — but as she did so, something caught Thuan's eye above the ruined rooftops of the shrine. A flash of dark paper, flapping in the wind. "Wait," he said.

It *was* a fragment of paper charm, caught in the air. No. No. The children. Asmodeus.

No. No.

"Wait," Thuan said, and started running.

There were more paper charms on the path, fluttering under the ruined three-arch gate that led into the outer courtyard — all singed with Fallen magic and littered over the paved stones, piled under the arches, spilling into the courtyard and stained with —

Blood. It was blood. Thuan's dragon senses were sharp enough to pick up on it, and it wasn't just any blood: it was the lazy, lambent blood of a wounded Fallen.

No no no.

He took the courtyard at a run, expanding into his dragon shape as he did so, summoning *khi*-water and ready to rain down the wrath of Heaven on anyone who'd dared to harm his husband, who'd dared to — the children, let the children be safe.

He found Asmodeus against one of the pillars at the entrance to the shrine, pinned to the mouldy lacquer by a sword, the entry wound — straight below his ribs on the left side, just below the scar he had, the long one Thuan had traced so many times when they were in bed together — oozing blood all over the fine linen of his shirt. He was sitting over a carpet of singed charms, the stones around him charred and melted by bursts of Fallen magic. His face was pale, his eyes closed, his glasses hanging askew on his face, the lenses smeared with charred ashes and blood. His knives were on the floor, bloodied up to the hilt, the paper charms closest to them slashed to pieces and inert.

"Asmodeus? Asmodeus!" He didn't answer when Thuan called out, or move — or when Thuan shook him — except that he flopped on the nearby coral, slightly, like a broken doll, and more blood flowed out. No no no. That wasn't possible. His husband was a force of nature. He'd almost died before, but surely he wouldn't find an ending here, of all places — not in some out of the way shrine to some unknown deity, not in the dragon kingdom he'd always hated. "Asmodeus. Please."

The children.

Where were the children?

Thuan let go of Asmodeus's body — his hands came away bloodied, with several charms sticking to them.

"Ai Nhi? Camille?"

Asmodeus would have tried to protect them — to the death, to this — this bleeding mess that made it hard for Thuan to breathe. Behind Thuan, a gasp: he turned, briefly, to see Quang Thu stare in horrified fascination at Asmodeus's limp body. Diem Chau, face set, was already kneeling by Asmodeus's side, her fingers, sheening with the orca's rubbery skin, looking for the pulse. He was alive, if he was bleeding. Dying, perhaps, but he had to be alive. And Thuan couldn't worry about any of this, because if Asmodeus ever woke up and found out that Thuan had put Asmodeus's well-being over that of the children, he was going to give Thuan the world's most pointed and most unpleasant verbal flaying — and to be honest, Thuan would have entirely deserved it.

Think. If he'd been Asmodeus and under attack, he'd most definitely have stashed the children somewhere hard to reach. The shrine was exposed, and with charms raining down, the skies weren't an option — and Asmodeus couldn't fly with Thuan absent. But the shrine deepened from building into cave, where the charms would have a much harder time not getting caught on random bits of rock or statuary.

Thuan went into the darkness of the shrine, cautiously wedging his dragon body through the opening — one of his small forelegs holding up a blue flame of *khi*-water.

"Ai Nhi? Camille? It's all right, I'm back. You're safe."

Asmodeus would also have told them not to move under pain of punishment, and Ai Nhi was smart enough to know when to obey him. That had to be the reason why nothing seemed to be moving in the darkness of the shrine.

Ancestors, please. Please let them be alive. Please let them be safe. Thuan wove a simple spell to find eddies in the currents of *khi*-water: a way to find if a dragon was nearby and within reach. Its range was not much larger than his field of vision, and it wasn't accurate, but in his state of stress he didn't trust himself to be able to look for fine details.

"Come out, please. It's Unka Thuan. I brought a healer, and the charms are gone."

There.

Movement, behind the broken statue with its pock-marked face. "Children?"

There was some kind of hurried argument, in voices he couldn't quite make out. Then: "Unka Thuan!", and before he knew it Camille was *jumping* at him with such energy and strength that his head went sideways. "Unka Thuan Unka Thuan—"

Ai Nhi's approach was more cautious: she slid out

from behind the legs of the statue in dragon shape, looking right and left, with a defensive weave of *khi*-water around her. "Unka Thuan?"

Thank Heaven. "It's all right," Thuan said, feeling a very large knot come undone in his belly. "It's all right." And he wrapped himself around both of them, breathing in their presence. "Are you unharmed?"

Ai Nhi grimaced, her maw displaying white, sharp fangs, her teal mane shimmering in the dim light. She held out her stubby arm, with a thin bloodied gash just below her elbow. "One of them got me, but I incinerated it with *khi*-water!"

"That's good," Thuan said, breathing out.

"And Unka Asmo did tell me to stab the men if they got into the cave, but no one did." Ai Nhi sounded almost disappointed.

"There were too many bad men," Camille said, her round face serious.

"Yes," Thuan said. "And it's good they didn't come in," Thuan said, and then his brain caught up with his heart. "Why did they not come with — Lan. Where is Lan?" Even as he asked, he knew the answer.

"She didn't come in," Ai Nhi said. She looked crestfallen.

Camille said, brightly, "She's with Unka Asmo, isn't she? He'll protect her."

"Your unka isn't really in a state to protect anyone right now," Quang Thu said, behind Thuan. She was standing at the entrance to the shrine, limned in the light from outside. "Come outside, children. It'll be better in the light. It's safe."

Diem Chau's voice floated into the darkness. "Big'bro, come out. I know you. You're going to stay in the dark and fret. It's no place for either you or the children."

"How is he?" Thuan asked.

"I'll tell you when you're outside," Diem Chau said.

"Is Unka Asmo hurt?" Ai Nhi said, even as Camille started wailing. "No, lil'sis, no. It's all right. Don't be scared, it's all right."

"Let's get out," Thuan said, gently carrying the crying Camille and Ai Nhi still trying to hug her — and wondering how in ten hells he was going to not cry himself. "We'll talk about it afterwards."

Outside, Diem Chau had removed the sword from Asmodeus's body, but left him against the pillar. She'd also taken away his glasses, which she'd cleaned and put on the steps by his side. She'd unrolled her kit on the floor and was busy putting acupuncture needle after acupuncture needle into his body, sucking on her teeth as she did so. Next to her kit was a cup of tea and a small teapot. Thuan wasn't sure how she'd gotten it going, but he could smell the tea: mineral, with a faint hint of grass.

She'd woven a complex net of *khi*-water over Asmodeus, and was busy adding to it with every needle, until it seemed Asmodeus was awash in blue light. His eyes were still closed, his face sallow and drained of the light that usually permeated Fallen. He looked almost unnnatural without his usual sarcastic expression, as if he were sleeping but not looking the way he should in repose — always one step away from waking up and stabbing someone in a single fluid gesture. It was *wrong.*

"They have Lan, then." Thuan said. "Lil'sis."

"Mmm," Diem Chau said.

Quang Thu was clearing paper charms from the shrine, muttering darkly under her breath as each one hit the coral and rock on the floor. Then she sat down to cast some kind of spell, looking downright annoyed. A shimmering dome sprang between her outstretched hands, slowly growing larger and larger until it encompassed the whole shrine. "There," she said. "That should hold against charms."

"You had one over the shrine before. When you left for the ministry," Thuan said, slowly, carefully. He was upset and worried and the last thing he wanted was to take it out on her.

"Yes, I did," Quang Thu said. "Throw enough charms at it and it'll break. The amount of power Khac Anh sank into this is immense. I don't understand why." She took out papers from her sleeves, spread them on the ground. "But that son of a demon is not going to get away with it." She made a movement with her sleeves. "Go look at your husband and reassure the children. I've got this."

"But—" Thuan said.

"No buts." Quang Thu said. "I failed you on this one. I'm not going to fail a second time."

Which left Thuan holding two anxious and crying children while Diem Chau was working, and desperately trying to think of a way to reassure them that wouldn't involve lying or making promises he couldn't keep. Really, unclehood wasn't all it was cracked out to be.

"Unka Thuan?" Ai Nhi asked. He'd finally gotten them to calm down by singing them songs, and Camille had fallen asleep, sucking on her thumb and shivering, wrapped within the curve of Thuan's dragon body. "Are the bad men going to come back?"

"You're scared they might?" Thuan said.

Ai Nhi said, "The sky just went dark with those charms, and then those people came out of nowhere with swords. Unka Asmo screamed at us to get into the cave, and he started fighting them, but there were so many..." She shivered. "After a while, we just didn't hear anything anymore. But what if they hadn't left? So we stayed there." She stared at Asmodeus's pale face. "If we'd come out earlier, maybe he wouldn't be hurt."

Thuan hugged her. "You did the right thing. I know you're feeling guilty because you wanted to help. But you'd be dead. Or captured with Lan." If Lan was even still there anymore, and not exorcised.

Ai Nhi didn't look happy — and it was the hardest thing, that Thuan had to live with her fear and her upset, unable to fix any of it. "Are you all right?" Ai Nhi asked.

Thuan weighed answers, and the only thing that came out was the truth. "No. I'm angry and scared." And feeling like a failure. Was the little information they'd got worth leaving Asmodeus alone with the children? If he hadn't been off, if Quang Thu had been there...

Ai Nhi hugged him. "It's all right to be scared," she said, and Thuan felt as though his heart would burst.

A sound made him look up, his large muzzle scattering droplets of *khi*-water around the courtyard. A deep, shuddering breath from Asmodeus. Diem Chau sat back on her haunches, not letting go of her spell. She watched him — and so did Thuan, with a painful and fragile hope rising in his chest, wringing his lungs and guts at the same time.

Asmodeus's eyes opened, light flowing back into his skin. He sat up straighter — needles scattering as he moved. His hands found the knives on the floor, slipped them back into his sleeves — and his glasses, which he put on by touch. His gaze, moving, found Thuan's held it. He breathed out, slowly, carefully, and some of the tension left him. "Good. You're alive."

"Unka Asmo!"

"Child," Asmodeus said, sternly. He tried to pull himself up, but Diem Chau's hands pushed him down.

"Don't move," she said, sternly. "You'll bleed out if you do. Give it..." she frowned. "Another hour. Your Fallen magic should have knitted your wound back together by then."

Asmodeus's gaze turned her. "And you are?"

Diem Chau bowed to him, her orca shape barely visible — except her eyes, small and beady, and a slight sheen in her hair. "Thuan brought me."

"Ah." Something sparkled in Asmodeus' gaze. "You're his ex-lover."

"And you're his husband. Diem Chau. I'm an apothecary in the Cinnabar Sea dispensary."

"Asmodeus. Co-head of House Hawthorn," he said. "You already know, I assume. Honoured. My thanks for the healing."

"Don't mention it," Diem Chau said. "It was for Thuan's sake."

"Was it." They were gazing at each other, sizing each other up in a way that really, really shouldn't have made Thuan more nervous — for Heaven's sake, his husband was alive and breathing and all he was worried about was how he and Diem Chau would get on?

Finally Asmodeus smiled. "Another hour, you said."

"Unless you want to spectacularly bleed to death. I don't particularly care, but I think Thuan would find it upsetting."

"He's always been soft-hearted," Asmodeus said.

"I'm pretty sure you'd have been upset too if I'd been the one pinned to a pillar with a sword," Thuan burst out.

"Oh, I'd have killed everyone involved in hurting you in extremely slow and creative ways," Asmodeus said, matter of factly. "Told you: you're the soft-hearted one out of the two of us."

"Asmodeus!" Thuan said, pointing to Ai Nhi.

Asmodeus rolled his eyes. "You think she doesn't know what I'd do?" And, before Thuan could comment, to Ai Nhi, "You did well, hiding in the cave. And protecting your little sister." His eyes narrowed. "Where is Lan?"

"Can you still feel her?" Thuan asked.

"Yes," Asmodeus said. He sighed. Thuan recognised the signs: he was angry at himself for failing, and looking for someone to take it out on, preferably one of the people involved in hurting him. "I take it they got what they wanted. And apparently they wanted her alive."

"Which is good," Quang Thu said, kneeling in the midst of the papers she was reading. "We don't know what they want with her yet, but that she's alive is good. Because you won't survive if she's exorcised."

Because they were tied to each other. Thuan quelled the wave of anger that rose through him with difficulty. "Can't you unbind them?"

"Not without Lan," Quang Thu said. She spread her hands.

Great. Great. Thuan took a deep breath. "All right. Can we wait a little bit before we start talking? I'm going to need a moment of quiet here, and you're obviously going to need more time before you can walk."

"Mmm," Asmodeus said. "A little moment only. They took Lan alive. That doesn't mean they intend to keep her that way, and the more we tarry, the more unsafe she is."

Unsafe. Like Lan dying was the problem here — as opposed to his own life being in danger, which he was throwing away as easily as if it were a paper charm. Thuan exploded. "It's not 'alive'. She's a ghost!"

Asmodeus glared at him, gaze withering. "Is this really the conversation you want to be having now?"

"Ah ah ah," Diem Chau said. "An hour before serious quarrelling please."

Thuan breathed out, trying to calm himself. "Fine. I'll come back in a bit." And went off, seething, before he could say the irreparable.

When he came back — in human shape and with his anger back to simmering at the back of his mind — Thuan found Asmodeus standing against the pillar, chatting with Diem Chau, with Ai Nhi clinging to his now pristine trousers and Camille still asleep, curled up where Thuan had left her. Thuan was pretty sure they hadn't had time to grab extra clothes when they'd fled the palace, which meant that someone had used a cleaning spell. The bloodied shirt was on the paved floor, amidst the fragments of charms: Asmodeus had a new tight tunic of Viet make, of uncertain provenance. Diem Chau, probably.

Diem Chau was sipping at her tea. She smiled at him when she saw him. "You're here. Good. Your husband is healed. Mostly."

"Mostly?"

"Bar the issue of the ghost feeding on me," Asmodeus said. He'd straightened out his glasses, too: he looked composed and in control, as if he were in his own office and not in a preoccupying situation.

Trust him to use exactly the most wounding words. Thuan clenched his hands, trying to not scream at Asmodeus. Focus. He needed to focus on something, anything. Logical explanations for things would have to do. "Quang

Thu, you said there was a mention of Khac Anh and his guild of exorcists in those papers."

"Yes. Here," Quang Thu said. She handed Thuan a handful of pages written in forceful Southern characters.

Thuan stared at them. Letters blurred and skipped: too much anxiety from him. He read through them, but the words kept slipping out of his grasp. "Can you give me the gist?"

"Oh. Yes," Quang Thu said. "You were wondering at the link between the guild of exorcists and the Anemone Immortal." She flipped through the pages. "Here. There's someone called Khac Anh, a young exorcist. He fell in love with her, and beseeched, not her favour, but her attention."

Thuan felt his heart sink. "How long ago?"

"Two hundred years, give or take," Quang Thu said. "I assume it didn't work, because he's not mentioned anymore."

"No," Thuan said. "It didn't work, and he felt slighted, and now he wants to erase every single trace of her from this world. Her shrine. Her cult. Her, if he can reach her. And it's been two hundred years. If it wasn't so before, it's become an obsession." The kind of man Diem Chau had described — angry, entitled, controlling — probably would never forgive a no. "That's why people keep dying in the shrine. That's also why it's in such a bad state. It's been defaced."

"You think she's dead?" Quang Thu asked.

Thuan thought back to the shrine, to that odd sense of

impermanence. "I don't know. If she's not, she's in hiding. And her cult is clinging on to life by a thread."

"It's in pretty bad shape," Asmodeus said, from his place by the pillar. "And that doesn't explain why they took Lan. I doubt they took the life of every person who wandered into the shrine by accident."

"I think it might," Diem Chau said. "Remind me of the writing on Lan's body?"

"A prayer," Thuan said. "Wasn't it what you said?"

"*A handful of anemones by the side of the road, beasts on robes and flags fluttering in the breeze...*" Quang Thu said. A wind rose, gentle and soothing — it didn't touch any of the paper charms scattered on the floor, but simply laid ghostly fingers on Thuan's hair and shoulders, like a parent's caress or a teacher's proud touch.

"I've seen it," Thuan said. "In your papers."

"And it was over her whole body?" Diem Chau said.

"She seemed... to be made of it," Thuan said, and stopped. "You don't think—"

"I think Lan picked up something in the shrine," Diem Chau said. "A fragment of magic. Something linking her to the shrine, or to the immortal. Or both."

And Khac Anh was busy destroying every single remnant of the Anemone Immortal. Lan was in the way. Not just as a material witness, but as the holder of the magic she carried.

Asmodeus's face set. "So Khac Anh is going to kill her to dispel the immortal's magic."

And killing her would kill Asmodeus. Thuan took a

deep, shaking breath. "We have to stop him."

"For once, I agree," Asmodeus said.

"Exorcising her isn't going to be trivial," Quang Thu said. "She's not a stray ghost, and she's bound—"

Asmodeus gestured to his chest — where the sword had stabbed him, the wound would now be closed, knitted together by a Fallen's innate magic. "To me?"

"You're holding her in this world."

"So if they attempt to exorcise her, I'm going to feel it?" He sounded... curious, but there was an edge to it. Thuan recognised it: it was the head of House Hawthorn, about to lose one of his dependents. Asmodeus had never stood for anything like that. He had laid down his life rather than see that of the people he was responsible for endangered. It was... commendable, except that Thuan was deathly scared at the thought of losing him.

"Do you remember how much tying your life to her hurt?" Quang Thu said. "This'll be worse."

Asmodeus considered that, chewing on it as though it was a morsel of red meat. "My pain threshold is quite high. Do you have painkillers?" he asked Diem Chau.

Diem Chau gave him a sharp look. Grudging approval. "You're Fallen. I don't know how fast your body metabolises drugs. But I can give you a few things that wouldn't majorly affect your motor control."

"Good. A few precautions wouldn't hurt."

Definitely the head of House Hawthorn. Except Lan wasn't even a dependent. She was a bloodthirsty ghost he'd decided was a child and treated as such in spite of the available evidence. Thuan bit his lips. "You could also stay here while we go retrieve Lan."

"Would you, if the situation was reversed?"

Touché. "No," Thuan said.

"Besides, there's not enough of us."

"I don't know even know what we're doing. Or when."

"Figure out where she is. Go get her," Asmodeus said.

It sounded rather simple, except it wasn't.

"Wherever they're holding her, it's going to be somewhere full of people and charms, and certainly not a place you gain admittance to just by asking."

Asmodeus put on his gloves slowly and deliberately, a gesture that looked much like a preliminary to drawing multiple knives. "Oh, I'm not planning on asking."

"Do you even have a plan?" Thuan said, forcing himself to enunciate words slowly and clearly, because the alternative would have been yelling at Asmodeus again, and that was pointless, with his life running out with every passing moment.

Someone nudged him. It was Ai Nhi, in dragon shape. "No fighting," she said in a small voice. "Unka..."

Thuan sighed. "All right. Sorry. I'm tense. And not thinking clearly. Now that we know who's the culprit, we could arrest Khac Anh, with the militia at our back."

"Yes," Diem Chau said. "If you have about five bi-hours to spare to argue with your aunt, your cousin and the head of the militia, in that order and not necessarily an exhaustive list, that you want to arrest Khac Anh and that the urgency is on account of the kidnapping of a ghost."

A ghost the court would care little about. He'd seen Hong Chi's face.

"A ghost tied to Asmodeus. Surely—" Thuan started, and then stopped. In the Dragon Court, Asmodeus was nothing but an interloper who'd had the good fortune to become Thuan's husband.

"Surely they'd be quite happy to see me dead," Asmodeus said. His smile was wide and easy, utterly sarcastic. "Your aunt could marry you again to someone more politically expedient. Perhaps the head of another House. Perhaps Shellac. I hear they have quite an extensive library."

"I can see why you're so popular," Thuan said, drily.

"Not now," Diem Chau said, her face the orca one, large enough to swallow them all whole, and looking distinctly peeved. "One step at a time. Asmodeus is right. Where would she be held?"

"The guild or the villa." Thuan frowned. "Not the guild. It's too blatant, and he's been careful about obscuring his involvement so far. Every murder looked like a separate one."

"Oh, and sending a thousand paper charms into the imperial palace wasn't blatant?" Asmodeus asked.

"This is a person who's been serially murdering people, so I don't think subtlety is his strong suit." Thuan sighed. "All right. Let's scope out the villa and figure out how to get into it fast, then. What are we doing with the children?"

Asmodeus smiled. "Why, finding a babysitter."

"Unka," Ai Nhi said, pouting.

"Babysitter," Asmodeus said, firmly. "And no sneaking out to find us or I'll be very cross with you."

"What your unka means is that it's dangerous and that someone needs to keep an eye on Camille."

Ai Nhi made a face. "The babysitter can."

"No," Thuan said. He looked for a reasonable thing to say, gave up, and decided to take a leaf out of Asmodeus's book. "Look, your unka is right. We're both going to be very cross and very sad if anything happens to you."

Ai Nhi sighed. "No fun," she said, but she nodded.

Asmodeus grinned, and for a brief moment Thuan wanted to kiss him. "Diem Chau?" Asmodeus asked. "You said you had a dispensary? How trustworthy is it?"

Diem Chau sighed. "I can find someone reliable there."

"Someone other than you? You're coming with us?" Thuan asked. He opened his mouth again, to say she couldn't possibly risk her life, and met Asmodeus's steady and utterly serious gaze.

Diem Chau's face was human again, with just the two white dots on either cheek, and her gaze was pitying. "Thuan, you'll be dead in two hours if I don't come with you."

"Me?" Thuan said.

Diem Chau pointed to Asmodeus. "He knows exactly what he wants and he's utterly focused on what to do to get it. You're full of stress and worry, and it'll be a wonder if you don't explode in flight."

"Charmed," Asmodeus said, but the worst thing was that he did sound charmed.

"You're a healer," Thuan said, desperately.

"With a patient in danger," Diem Chau said, gesturing to Asmodeus. She gestured again with her sleeves, and came out with three acupuncture needles between each finger, glistening with fluid. "You'll find I can be rather focused on what to do when the safety of people under my care is at stake."

Silence. Then short, amused laughter from Asmodeus. "You mean Thuan has a type?"

"Thuan *absolutely* has a type," Diem Chau said.

"I'm right here," Thuan said. Being teased simultaneously by his husband and his ex had definitely not been on the to-do list for today.

"Oh, I know," Diem Chau said. She smiled, and the needles were back in her sleeves.

"So you're coming as my babysitter?"

"Think of it as moral support. With backup needles to incapacitate guards. Besides, Khac Anh isn't playing fair. Ten of thousands of paper charms?"

Something Quang Thu had said needled at Thuan. "Quang Thu? You did say you had a way to send these back to their owner?" A mass of paper charms would certainly qualify as a large distraction.

"Yes," Quang Thu said. "I do."

"And how long is it going to take you to rewrite the charms?"

"The time it's going to take you to have a look at that villa," Quang Thu said.

"I've been there before. I'll take you there," Diem Chau

said. "Let's go. We'll drop off the children on our way."

"Well," Thuan said.

They were crouching behind a coral rise, a few measures away from Khac Anh's villa. Behind them, Quang Thu was still writing on a mass of inert charms: she was almost finished but seemed to be fiddling with something.

It was, Thuan supposed, better than the guild, if one were to pick a place to attack: a series of steps leading up to a large door, a large courtyard behind it where various people looked to be training, and then the private quarters behind it, a series of other smaller courtyards with ponds and gardens in their centre. There were no particular fortifications.

"Still keen on walking in?" Thuan asked.

Asmodeus had a knife in his gloved hand, which seemed like nothing so much as an extension of him. "Into wherever Lan is held, yes."

"That's him," Diem Chau said, sharply.

A group of people who looked like a small army was walking up the path leading to the villa, carrying a wooden palanquin whose carvings were all worn and overgrown with algae. "In the palanquin?" Thuan said.

"Yes."

Thuan watched the people guarding the palanquin: they had swords, stood up ramrod-straight, and around them were various protective weavings of *khi*-water.

Professionals, and that was before the paper charms he could see atop the palanquin and the rooftops. He almost wished they had Lan: she'd have made short work of the charms.

The person who left the palanquin was almost disappointingly ordinary: a tall, stocky dragon in human shape with elegant antlers and the faint shadow of a moustache on his face. But when he moved, Thuan saw it: this was someone who expected the world to move with him. He glanced at his guards, and it was even clearer that he'd consider anyone who didn't follow his exact orders a traitor. Someone who wasn't used to hearing no, Diem Chau had said. His eyes were dark and deep-set in a round, moon-shaped face, his posture easy, relaxed. He made other people tense. That was the whole point of it.

"Khac Anh," he said.

"Yes," Asmodeus said. His gaze was sharp, weighing. Considering, and Thuan was pretty sure it was all about ways to hurt Khac Anh as much as Khac Anh had hurt Asmodeus — not physically, but by threatening the people Asmodeus cared for.

Khac Anh was talking to one of his guards. His round face relaxed even further. He smiled, and it was an utterly unpleasant expression. "He knows they have her." Thuan said.

Asmodeus's hand was tense on his knife. "Yes. And that's not the face of a man who's going to be *nice* to her." His voice was dripping with sarcasm — barely masked anger.

No. It was the face of a man who was going to take delight in hurting someone else. A child. Thuan felt a physical revulsion. "All right," Thuan said. "Which way in? Not the front door."

"Where is she being held?" Asmodeus asked.

Diem Chau frowned. She was drinking tea from the cup she'd withdrawn from her sleeves: a darker, nuttier oolong. Thuan was impressed by her capacity to get tea made in any circumstances. "The cells are below the villa. The entrance is there, in that courtyard with the black bridge over the green coral pond."

It was just behind the first courtyard.

"I admit you might have a point," Asmodeus said. "We're not going to walk in."

Oh, good. Thuan didn't have time to say it before Asmodeus said, "We're going to fly in."

"With those charms?"

"The charms are going to be busy with Quang Thu's little army," Asmodeus said.

"Asmodeus, we're meant to *survive* going in. A little tactical awareness —"

"— is irrelevant."

For him, maybe. The same thing, again and again — failing to consider his life had any worth at all, so easily sacrificing it. And all for. A ghost. A creature that only survived because it killed the living. Thuan bit his lip. "Well, since I'm apparently in charge. Quang Thu can send the charms through the main courtyard. Do you need to be guiding them?"

"No," Quang Thu said. "They'll be making for their maker, but in the meantime they'll provide a very large distraction."

"So you could also be knocking on their front door and asking embarrassing questions," Thuan said.

Quang Thu looked startled. "As a magistrate?"

"Yes," Thuan said. "If you're willing."

"They won't kill me," Quang Thu said. Her face was grim. "They probably won't let me in, either."

"After the confusion starts? It's going to be much easier to slip in."

Quang Thu chewed on this for a while, her antlers shimmering in and out of existence. "All right. I'll see what I can do."

Diem Chau said, "That's a big pile of charms. Are you hoping they'll have fewer of these?"

"They will have fewer," Quang Thu said. "These are easy. They're to find a ghost. The more complex warding ones take longer to make."

"Any tips on how to avoid them?" Thuan asked.

"Fly fast," Quang Thu said. She pointed to Asmodeus. "Also, blast them out of the sky."

Asmodeus raised the knife he was holding a fraction — his equivalent of a nod. "I'm going to need those painkillers now," he said to Diem Chau. Diem Chau nodded, and took him away from the group.

Which left Thuan and Quang Thu.

Quang Thu said, slowly and carefully, "It's not my business, but... you haven't really had a chat with him, have you?"

"Is it that painfully obvious?" Thuan asked.

"That you're avoiding each other? Yes. And I wouldn't comment, but you're going to need to work together if you want to rescue Lan."

"I don't want to help her," Thuan said. He was surprised and a little ashamed at how easily it slipped out.

"I presume it's not about the danger to Asmodeus."

"No," Thuan said. "You know what it's about. Surely you don't approve of ghosts hanging around either."

Quang Thu's face was a mask — and unfortunately Thuan was too good at reading people not to notice she was refraining from making a comment. "Whatever it is you think I don't want to hear, I'd rather hear it now."

Quang Thu cocked her head, ghostly antlers shimmering into existence around her topknot. "Do you?" A sigh. "You asked me to look into murders in the shrine. I also looked for the ones around the shrine."

Thuan's heart sank. "The ones Lan would have committed to feed herself."

"There are two," Quang Thu said. "Over a period of fifty years. That's not a hungry ghost."

"She still killed people," Thuan said. "Drained them dry of their blood to sustain herself."

"And what about your husband? Did he not kill people?"

Thuan breathed out. "It's not the same thing! And you said it yourself. It'll get worse."

Quang Thu was silent, for a while. "Maybe it's not the

same thing. I can tell you this: this is almost unheard-of self-control. And yes, in the current situation, it will get worse. But—"

"But?"

"Who says you have to accept the current situation?"

Thuan stared at her. He opened his mouth. Closed it, because he didn't have a good answer. "I guess I have my limits on the amount of monstrousness I can tolerate," he said. "Can we please stop talking about it?" But he felt small and petty.

"As you wish," Quang Thu said.

Asmodeus and Diem Chau were walking back towards them, deep into some kind of conversation. Thuan thought it was about painkillers until he realised that the subject of the talk was rather different.

"And so he stabbed you?" Diem Chau was saying. "I'm having a hard time imagining Thuan stabbing anyone in cold blood, least of all his husband."

"It was a rather different situation," Asmodeus smiled. "To be fair, I was going to kill him at the first opportunity."

"Well," Diem Chau said. "That's certainly a novel way to start a relationship."

Thuan coloured. Stabbing Asmodeus — in self-defence, an act he'd done six years ago, back when his marriage to Asmodeus had still been an arranged and conflictual one, as opposed to the partnership it had turned into — wasn't necessarily the moment in his life he was proudest of. "Are you just trying to embarrass me?"

Asmodeus raised an eyebrow. "You're too attached to

old beliefs and old events, dragon prince." There was an edge to it, and it wasn't even a subtle dig.

"As opposed to you?" Thuan said. "Not attached enough to your life, I guess?"

Asmodeus raised his other eyebrow. "You were the one who was going to throw his away, back when Quang Thu asked for someone to link to Lan."

"And you're the one who took that decision away from me!"

"So you'd have made the same one, then!"

"I wouldn't have taken it that far! And now—" Thuan breathed in. No, he knew exactly what he was going to say next, and they couldn't afford that particular fight. He was going to say that now they had to go into a heavily guarded villa to rescue a ghost Thuan didn't care for, and he didn't need premonition to figure out that was a disastrous idea that would turn the simmering tension between them into a conflagration. "No," he said. "Let's go. I'm done with this."

"Good," Asmodeus said. "Because I don't see the point of having that conversation."

"You certainly shouldn't be having it that way," Diem Chau said. "Thuan is right. We need to go. You can sort out it out afterwards."

Thuan tried to forget his deepest worry — that by the time they rescued Lan, there would be no sorting out possible between them.

Waiting was more nerve-wracking than actually going in. Thuan lay in dragon shape, just out of sight of the charms on the walls, Asmodeus and Diem Chau on his back. He felt the presence of his husband — roiling warmth, that small and deliberate way Asmodeus had of shifting, the precise and controlled movements, the coiled focus.

"Do you think the children are asleep?" he asked.

A snort from Asmodeus. "I doubt it. We'll be lucky if Ai Nhi doesn't make a break for it with Camille in tow."

"Surely she's understood," Thuan started. "Well, at least how angry you're going to be at her."

"She cares a lot more about helping," Asmodeus said, and he sounded grudgingly admiring.

Thuan felt a tug on the nearby *khi*-currents — a sound, like a fluttering in the breeze. "That's Quang Thu," he said.

On his back, Diem Chau tensed, doing something he couldn't see but which shifted her weight. Asmodeus's knees just gripped Thuan's scales tighter. "Hold on," Thuan said. "This is going to be a really bumpy ride."

Distant snatches of sound: surprise, fear, panic. More fluttering, like banners unfolding. Thuan took off, bracing himself against the inevitable onslaught of charms — as his body went up, the wall of the villa descended, and his head was soon poking over the rooftop.

Where were all the charms?

Inside, it was sheer chaos: the courtyard was flooded by Quang Thu's own charms — she'd written over them in silver ink, and they were easy to separate from the other, darker paper ones entangled with them. Guards were screaming at each other to do something. Thuan caught a fast glimpse of the first courtyard as he dove towards the building Diem Chau had pointed to — a similar mess, and he could make out Quang Thu's voice, patiently and calmly making inquiries a flustered guard was attempting to answer.

Good.

Thuan landed in a heap on the floor of the second courtyard, the flagstones scraping under the soft area of his belly. Asmodeus and Diem Chau slid down, just as the first charms spotted them and fluttered towards him. They'd hurt, if they hit him, the same way they had when he'd been wounded over the palace. Thuan fought the urge to make himself smaller and smaller.

Asmodeus shifted. Fallen magic blasted the first bunch of charms out of the sky.

"Big'bro. Change shapes. Now," Diem Chau said, firmly. Something nudged him: the palm of her hand against the bulk of his body.

Thuan changed. Just as his shape settled into human, Asmodeus grabbed him and propelled him forward, out of the way of the charms diving for him. His other hand threw something: a knife, which buried itself into the chest of an exorcist trying to reach them.

"Intruders!" A wild-eyed guard screamed — a few seconds before Diem Chau stuck a needle into his back — and his eyes suddenly glazed over and he fell, limp and unresponsive.

"Remind me never to anger you," Thuan said, staring at her.

Diem Chau grinned. "Just keep taking me out for dinner and we'll be fine, Thuan."

"Here," Asmodeus said, slipping something into Thuan's hand. "For the record, I do my utmost to respect your baffling approach of talking things through first, but I absolutely disapprove of showing up empty-handed to this kind of mission."

What? Wait. Thuan stared at the knife in his hand. "Asmodeus, you can't give me your weapon—"

Asmodeus turned to him, briefly — pupils uncannily dilated, face awash with light, amused anger in every line of his body. "Oh, dragon prince. Do you really think I don't have other knives with me?"

And then all three of them were running across the black bridge — dodging and cutting and burning paper charms, towards the darkened entrance Diem Chau voicelessly pointed out. Thuan felt in the eye of a storm — a whirlwind of fighting charms around him, the *khi*-currents saturated with spells. A charm dove towards him — he slashed at it seconds before it could wrap itself around his wrist. Asmodeus was flinging Fallen magic left and right. In the other courtyard, Quang Thu's voice had fallen silent, and there was the sound of fighting. Good. She was trying to get in.

There were two guards at the entrance to the underground cells: they fell to Diem Chau's needles. Thuan had never seen her that way, lithe and incandescent and utterly deadly rather than the soft-spoken healer he'd dated — or rather, she was bringing the same passion and anger she reserved for people who made morally dubious choices, except she was physically taking it out on the guards. It... certainly made him think.

A ramp, leading down; torches of blue light that wavered in the rippling atmosphere of the dragon kingdom; more guards — Thuan didn't even have time to see Asmodeus move before they fell, knife in their throats, and then Asmodeus was moving to retrieve the knives from them. He flipped up the blades in a single fluid gesture, the handles settling into the palm of his hands, heedless of the blood that splattered onto his already bloodied gloves. He paused, for a single moment, wincing.

"Asmodeus?"

Asmodeus shook his head. "I'll be fine," he said, but Thuan realised he wasn't. That he hadn't been for a while. It wasn't just anger that was making him this incandescent — but a pain so great he shouldn't have been able to stand.

"He's exorcising her, isn't he."

Asmodeus gave him a look that could have melted stone. "I'm not going to talk about it. Let's move."

That wasn't good. As Asmodeus had said — his pain threshold was quite high, and he was already on Diem Chau's drugs. If he was impaired already, it wasn't going to get any better. Thuan shook his head, trying to dispel the ever-persistent sense of worry.

Khac Anh's charms had vanished, but the flood of Quang Thu's charms was still there — pushing against

Thuan's back, sliding between his legs and making straight for a door at the far end of the corridor. It was a large, two-panel one in a semi-circle shape, one of its panels half-open, magic spilling out from underneath the slit between threshold and the panels.

"That way," Thuan said, his voice echoing under the stone ceiling. To their right was a row of gates with rusted metal grating — cells, and most of them were occupied by live people.

"Focus," Asmodeus said, sharply, his hand gripping Thuan's shoulder and squeezing — and a softer touch from his magic, gently tugging Thuan's face away from the cells. "This isn't the time for distractions."

"We could help—"

"What was it you said? Tactical awareness. We don't have much time if we want to survive this. Go in, retrieve Lan. Go out."

Thuan shook his head. "My being distracted, no. But we could definitely use other people being distracted." He wove *khi*-water into cold ice, and drove it into the locks of the cells, again and again. "We took care of the guards," he said. "You're going to want to get out."

And then he jogged away, towards that huge door at the back.

The doors splintered open: Thuan heard the sharp sound of metal falling apart, and hesitant footsteps. He turned, briefly, to make sure the prisoners were making for the exit rather than following them, and then turned back to the door.

Asmodeus had already pushed it open and slipped inside.

Typical.

Diem Chau was by his side, breathing hard. They looked at each other: Thuan pointed towards the door. "Might as well," he said.

Before he gets himself killed.

"We could also get killed," Diem Chau said, echoing Thuan's unsaid thoughts. "Come on."

Thuan turned, to look at the corridor, and felt a faint presence: Quang Thu's *khi*-water, coming from the courtyard. She was in, but it was going to take her time to come. He sighed, and followed Diem Chau in.

Inside, it was blindingly light. Thuan thought for a moment he'd set foot in some version of the Heavenly City all Fallen yearned for — everything around him was radiance, so much he could barely see Diem Chau. Asmodeus was ahead of him: Thuan couldn't exactly see him but he could feel Asmodeus's dark, forceful presence. His feet crunched on something, a sound he'd have known anywhere.

Bones.

"You see," a voice said, from within the light, "she wasn't very nice." It was low-pitched, rich and cultured: the accents and language of the court, a voice one would immediately trust.

"Nice." It was Asmodeus's voice, seconds before he stabbed someone. Or everyone.

"I would have given her the world and everything in

it. She was beautiful and when she laughed, my heart just felt too large for my chest. But she said no."

Thuan's eyes adjusted to the light. Now he could see the room: it was circular, with a depression in the middle of the floor, and an *am duong* teardrop pattern carved in algae-eaten stone. On top of it were two rows of trestle tables, all empty save for two. Khac Anh stood in the middle of these, his feet on the duong half of the pattern. One table held Lan — who was pinned to it by wooden nails, her eyes open and her face contorted in pain, the writing on her skin luminescent and writhing. Her skin was cracked like eggshells and the cracks getting wider and wider, as if she were about to burst into light. Her mouth was open, her entire body was taut and tensed in a primal scream, but nothing came out.

That wasn't right. That wasn't fair. That — Thuan couldn't get past the tight knot of sheer anger in his belly.

On the other table was another body, except this one was... faded. Like an ink drawing run under water, the contours wobbling, the features blurred, everything somehow less than it should have been. She wasn't pinned the way Lan was, but there was a wound in her chest which had bled a faint, blurred red on her clothes — and the thin face and garb were all too familiar. She had writing on her skin — the same one Lan had, except it was blurred and running: it had spilled underneath her and was dripping on the floor, drop after drop of dark, sheening ink.

"The Anemone Immortal," Thuan said, aloud. So she wasn't in hiding. She was dead. She had been dead for perhaps a long, long time.

"She wasn't nice," Khac Anh said, again. "I offered her prayers, and flowers, and incense, and she wouldn't even grant me the time for an incense stick to burn."

Asmodeus was standing on the edge of the stairs leading into the depression, which was unusual for him. Thuan would have expected him to charge in, especially given how distressed Lan seemed. Thuan could imagine the screams the magic was swallowing in his head, and it wasn't a pleasant feeling — he just wanted to storm in and *end* it all, kill or incapacitate Khac An before he could inflict further harm on anybody...

Then he saw the charms.

They were the ones Quang Thu had written over, and they were scattered all around the depression, as if it marked an invisible demarcation line. There were also three guards, but they were all dead — one with a Fallen knife, and two with Quang Thu's charms wrapped around their necks. Did Khac Anh have any other charms in the room? He would have. Had to.

"Thuan." It was Diem Chau's voice. She pointed to the outside of the circle.

Oh.

He hadn't seen the flags. There were five of them in a pentagonal shape: simple triangles of white cloth on poles, with the same handwriting as the charms that had been after them, a protective enclosure. *That* was what had Asmodeus stymied. He appeared to be studying the situation, though Thuan was starting to suspect — and worry — that he was also being slowed down by pain. Pain which was unlikely to get better.

Thuan poked at the line the flags were drawing. It yielded to his touch for a millimeter before it became as hard as diamond, scraping his fingers. He threw some *khi*-water at it, which it effortlessly absorbed: it shimmered blue for a bare moment, and then went invisible again. The flags continued to move in an unseen current, unaffected.

Right. What next?

When in doubt, go back to what Thuan did best.

So, talk.

"She wasn't nice, so you killed her." He kept his voice level. It took an effort — he did it because he had to. Because it was Asmodeus's life at stake. "And the shrine just... declined."

Khac Anh stared at Thuan. Thuan had expected to see some kind of.... insanity. Some kind of delusional thinking. But no, this was someone who was utterly sane — proud of himself and in utter control.

Thuan poked again at the barrier. Diem Chau was trying magic too, and she wasn't having any more success than he was having. It absorbed everything that they were throwing at it. Perhaps a more subtle weave?

Khac Anh said, "It takes work to make a decline. Rumours. Wounds. Murders. Something to gradually make people understand that this isn't a shrine you go to anymore, not if you want your prayers granted. To make them see how much bad luck she carries."

Thuan looked at the Anemone Immortal. How much had she suffered, and what had happened before she'd died? And did he want to know? He took a deep breath. "And now there's just the matter of the ghost, isn't there."

He met Asmodeus's eyes: his husband's face was taut, but it wasn't anger. It *was* pain.

They were running out of time. By Thuan's side, Diem Chau was looking at the flags, head cocked. She was out of ideas, and so was Thuan. Lan was still screaming soundlessly — and the writing on her skin was running out, too, more ink pooling on the table and on the floor, her features becoming blurrier and blurrier.

Fading away, and Asmodeus with her.

Keep talking. He knew Quang Thu was on his way. These were exorcists' flags. She'd know what to do when she did arrive.

Smile.

Keep talking, no matter how hard it was.

Khac Anh laughed, a sound that made Thuan's hair stand on end. "You're here for the *ghost*? Ghosts get exorcised. Guild business."

"Especially ghosts with the last remnants of the Immortal's magic," Asmodeus said. Thuan wasn't sure whether to be impressed, or appalled, that his husband's voice didn't shake, or even become less than utterly sarcastic and conversational. Asmodeus's tense grip on his knives was a dead giveaway that he wasn't at all fine. "Who knows, the cult might start up again."

"It won't." A flash of anger on Khac Anh's face. "It's

dead. Thai Ha was the last one. They won't come back. Not to an empty defaced shrine. But that's not enough. There shouldn't be anything of her left. Nothing she's touched. Nothing she's cared for. No magic."

"An admirable sentiment," Asmodeus said, gravely inclining his head. "Making examples is a commendable business. It's a pity you think it acceptable to make it at the expense of a child." One of his legs wobbled; he kept it locked for a moment, but then — biting his lip, he... he didn't kneel so much as slowly fold towards the floor.

Asmdoeus! Thuan's lips closed on what he wanted to say.

"Principles." Khac An moved, to stand over Lan — straightening the nail in her upper arm. Lan writhed, buckled, trying to escape. Khac Anh merely drove it deeper with the kind of smile that Thuan ached to smash from his face. "A pity they won't get you anywhere."

And abruptly Quang Thu was there too, taking in the situation and nodding abruptly. "The flags," Thuan said.

Quang Thu nodded again. She made a gesture with her sleeves, and charms came out — a different colour, vermilion instead of dark, going towards the flags. They toppled like limp puppets just at the same time as Asmodeus's second knee hit the ground, and his face — pale, limned in light, lips blood-red — twisted in an expression Thuan had never seen and didn't want to see again.

Thuan saw red.

He was down the steps, past the blasted protection wards, throwing himself on Khac Anh before he could think — and Khac Anh hadn't expected it, either, because he went down, with Thuan pummelling him over and over again — Khac Anh trying to dodge but Thuan was hitting him over and over, with the knife he barely remembered holding — Asmodeus's knife.

"Thuan!!" It was Diem Chau, hauling him off. Khac Anh was still down on the floor, bleeding and in no state to get up, let alone fight back. "Stop it."

Thuan breathed. "Why?"

"Because you're not a killer."

"That's my job," Asmodeus said, his voice floating from what felt like far away. "And you're terrible at this bit.... dragon... prince."

Khac Anh was lying in a puddle of blood. He smiled at Thuan — slow and arrogant. "Principles," he said. "If I'm dead, you won't escape this villa."

"He does have a point," Diem Chau said. "A hostage might be useful to not be killed by the rest of the guards."

Thuan took a deep, shaking breath. "Go see to Asmodeus."

"Thuan."

"Asmodeus," he said, firmly. The anger was still within every fibre of his body, so strong he could hardly breathe — a terrible way to make any kind of decision.

"For your information," Quang Thu said, "It's still chaos out there. Not many guards left alive, or who didn't run."

Which didn't really make killing Khac Anh fair. Though. Thuan thought of the Anemone Immortal, of her life being pulled apart little by little for no more reason than because she'd dared to say no to a man's obsession (he couldn't, wouldn't call it love).

Thuan turned, briefly. Diem Chau was kneeling by Asmodeus's side, putting needles in. Asmodeus's eyes were glazed now, and Thuan could hear his laboured breathing. In, out. In, out.

No time.

Thuan stared at Lan, on the trestle table, Lan, buckling and writhing — features blurring, sharp, wicked teeth in the oval of her face. There was no writing left now: just pale skin that kept getting more and more translucent. He could see the stone floor and the walls of the room through her.

A ghost. Feeding on blood. A creature of evil to be exorcised — and yet he could hear her scream at the back of his mind. He could taste her fear.

He wasn't sure what moved him, then. The gesture he reached for — away from the bleeding Khac Anh and towards the trestle table with Lan on it, towards the nails, pulling them out one by one — was one he'd have done anyway, to stop the exorcism. To save Asmodeus. Except... Except that there was something within him, like a muscle finally loosing — something that felt too large and too fragile for his chest.

Pity. He was sorry for her.

"It's all right," he said to Lan. "Just a couple more." He pulled out the last two nails — one in her lower belly and one in the hollow just below her neck — and Lan just...

flopped, straight into his arms.

She didn't feel like a living child, like Camille or Ai Nhi. But not like a corpse, either: Thuan had carried his fair share of those. She was cold, like the depths of sea, like the very end of the night, before sunrise. For a moment he held her and she stared up at him, and her eyes were awash with the handwriting on the shrine of the Anemone Immortal, and then that, too, faded, and she smiled, one clawed hand reaching for Thuan's cheek — he instinctively shied away, but she just laid it on his skin, and some of the cold rested there too, for a bare moment.

When she took it away, he felt as though he'd lost something infinitely precious.

"Is there any kind of emergency?" he asked.

Diem Chau slid a final needle into Asmodeus's lower belly. "No," he said. "He's stable, and the exorcism has been interrupted. They'll both hold for a while." She rose, propping Asmodeus up on her shoulder. "Can you walk?" she asked. "At least into the courtyard."

Asmodeus stared at her with the vacant eyes of someone who wasn't quite there. "Thuan?"

Thuan was having too many feelings and he wasn't quite sure how to sort them all out, so he settled for the time-honoured, self-destructive method of pretending they didn't exist. "I can carry him," he said, Lan's weight still in his arms. "I'll change here. Let's go before the guards can regroup. We can figure all this out once we're out of here."

"And him?" Quang Thu asked, pointing to Khac Anh — who was now unconscious from loss of blood, and pinned down by four of her charms.

"Him, too," Thuan said, firmly, adding 'murderous psychopath worse than my husband' somewhere at the end of the long list of issues he was going to have to deal with. He really, really wanted to curl up with a book and didn't think he was going to get a chance for a long, long time.

In the end, Khac Anh was the easiest one to handle: Thuan let Quang Thu take him and a full report, which he didn't have the energy for, to his cousin Hong Chi. At some point, it was all going to turn into a lecture from Hong Chi if he was lucky and his aunt the Empress if he wasn't. Asmodeus, who was still not entirely collected, went with a grimly determined Diem Chau — who all but threw Thuan out of the healing room with pointed references on the necessity to let her work, and didn't he have children to think of?

Thuan, still struggling to collect his thoughts, went to the dispensary, where he retrieved said children in an over-excited state.

"Unka Thuan! You're safe!" Ai Nhi said.

"And you stayed put," Thuan said. "I'm very impressed."

"We were very well-behaved," Ai Nhi said, proudly, and Thuan could see their babysitter behind Ai Nhi, grimacing and wordlessly voicing objections with a very eloquent set of expressions.

"I'm sure," he said.

"Did you get the bad men?" Ai Nhi asked.

"Yes."

"And Lan?"

Lan was with Quang Thu, or Asmodeus. Thuan was procrastinating on what to do, at least until Diem Chau was done healing Asmodeus. "We helped Lan out," Thuan said, finally. It was factual and true.

"That's good," Camille said. "Lan is nice."

Thuan bit his lip.

"Unka Thuan doesn't agree," Ai Nhi said, and Thuan just stood there feeling extremely guilty and unsure what to say. In the end, he gave up, and brought the children back to their quarters.

Their rooms had been cleaned up of the mess, though he found a handful of paper charms in the courtyard. Ai Nhi stared forlornly at the remnants of her drawings on the table: they had been burnt by Fallen magic and then rained on. "I'm very sad," she said.

"I know," Thuan said, and knelt and hugged both of them.

A knock at the door: Thuan opened it, and found Quang Thu, with Lan by her side. Quang Thu had changed into court robes, a full five-panel dress with many layers — though they were all plain cloth with no embroidery, and the roughest of weaves. Lan wore robes with dragons, something reserved for the children of the imperial family: her hair had been combed back into a tidy topknot, and her skin was once more pale rather than cracked. She smiled at Thuan, sharp-toothed and utterly happy, her hands making gestures.

She was happy to see him.

"I thought she shouldn't be alone," Quang Thu said.

"Lil'sis!" Ai Nhi shrieked when she saw Lan. "You're safe!"

Lan grinned, showing fangs. Camille ran up to her and gave her a hug, and then grabbed her hand. "Come on," she said, "Pillow fight!"

Lan looked to Thuan — her molten-silver gaze uncertain. Thuan sighed. "Go," he said. He heard the bedroom door slammed, and then the distant shrieking and laugher of children racing each other.

"Is she still — ?"

"Linked to your husband? Yes," Quang Thu said. "I'm not going to undo this until he's better. Not to mention consenting."

"What did Hong Chi say?" Thuan asked.

Ai Nhi's voice drifted through the door. "No, lil'sis, no. Not that way. When I tag you, you're it. You're the one who chases people."

A sound from Lan — not a screech but some kind of trill. Laughter, Thuan realised. She was laughing, and he realised he was smiling in return, before he remembered she was a ghost, and stopped.

"Hong Chi was not thrilled." Quang Thu's face was an interesting study in deliberate neutrality. "She said she's going to have the biggest mess to clean up on account of you two."

"We did solve the murder. Murders," Thuan said.

Quang Thu gave him a look that was pure Hong Chi. "I believe she said something about the death toll. And about the usual devastation in your husband's wake."

"It was really both of us," Thuan said with a grimace. "But she'll get over it?"

"I think so." Quang Thu withdrew a fan from her sleeves, and toyed with it, folding and unfolding it but never bringing it close to her face. "You're right that you did end up solving murders. Of officials. And of the Anemone Immortal."

Thuan thought of that blurred, indistinct silhouette on the trestle table. "She's gone then."

"Yes," Quang Thu said. "He killed her and exorcised her, as if she were a ghost. No one recovers from that. She'll get reborn, though I realise it's scant comfort."

"Everyone gets reborn when they're dead. And considering what happened to her? Not much comfort, no." Thuan pulled a chair, and sat down in it. The table was empty, and there didn't seem to be any tea anywhere. What he wouldn't have given for even Asmodeus's acrid, overbrewed concoctions. "And Khac Anh will get reborn too."

"Khac Anh is going to have to give a serious accounting before he can get anywhere near rebirth," Quang Thu said. "I was surprised you didn't suggest your husband handle him."

"I did consider it," Thuan said.

"And?"

"It was very tempting." Heaven knew Asmodeus would have more than a few ideas on how to make Khac Anh's last living hours a misery on so many people's accounts. "But it wouldn't have been fair."

"Ah. And you think he'll appreciate that?"

"In his own way." Thuan knew exactly what Asmodeus would say: if they hadn't been avoiding each other, he could even imagine the look Asmodeus would give him, that mixture of exasperation and fondness at Thuan's way of looking at things. He missed that with all his soul. "Speaking of fairness..."

"Yes?" Quang Thu asked.

"Can I ask you a question?"

"Yes."

"You said Lan needed to feed on people to survive. Why?"

"Ghosts need organs. Or blood. Something of the living." Quang Thu explained. "It's the way they remain in the world."

"That's not people though, is it? Does it have to involve her killing them?"

Quang Thu watched him for a while. "I suppose not," she said. "What did you have in mind?"

Thuan didn't really know if he had anything in mind. "I need to think," he said. "Can I talk to you and Hong Chi later?"

After Quang Thu left, Thuan went to put the children to bed. Which was... a challenge. Lan was subdued: she smiled at him entirely too much, which made him suddenly realise she was doing it because she was uncomfortable and unsure of how to fit in — which in turn fed the pit of unease in his own stomach, that slowly dawning realisation he might not have been entirely fair to Lan. "You like it here," he said to Lan.

Lan nodded. Her face blurred, but her eyes remained wide open, dark and quivering. Her skin was as white as porcelain, finely cracked and translucent.

"She wants to stay," Ai Nhi said, and Lan nodded.

Thuan took a deep breath. "Let's talk about something else for now," he said.

Ai Nhi was chatty, but they'd had a big couple of days, and she soon exhausted herself trying to talk to Thuan. Lan fell asleep like a log, possibly because of the abortive and interrupted exorcism being exhausting. Camille, unfortunately, was nervous and kept going out of her bed every ten minutes to ask for a cuddle. Thuan lost count of how many times he had to bring her back to bed, carefully trying not to let his exhaustion show. By the time the children were all asleep, Thuan was beyond worn out physically and emotionally. He fished his book out of the bedside table, and settled on the bed, his antlers leaning against the wood.

He must have slept, because when he woke up, it was dark, and someone had spoken his name.

"Thuan?"

It was Asmodeus, standing in the doorway of the bedroom. He was leaning on a cane, his grip on it too tight for it to be decorative. Thuan exhaled. "How are you?"

A shrug. "I've been worse."

Which wasn't an answer, but Thuan could guess.

"Lan—"

"In the bedroom," Thuan said. "She's asleep."

An exhalation. "I see. Thank you. The other children?"

"In bed too," Thuan said. "We can figure out what to tell everyone tomorrow."

Asmodeus nodded. He left his gloves — bloodied and torn — on the table at the entrance of the room, and picked up the cane again, walking to the bed. He sat down next to Thuan, head leaning against the wall — black hair haloed in Fallen light. His usual smell of bergamot and citrus was weaker, overwhelmed by camphor. "It's been suggested to me we should talk." His voice was stiff.

"Diem Chau?"

"She's quite single-minded. I can see why you like her." Asmodeus smiled, but it was an exhausted expression. "But not quite. You said I couldn't keep running away from hard conversations, once. Or making decisions for you. Consider this... an opening, to try and mend things."

Ah. Thuan didn't quite know what to do with that, either. "So Lan, then." This was... uncomfortable and new, like clothes that didn't quite fit. What had Quang Thu said?

It will only get worse in the current situation, but who says you have to accept it?

Thuan said, finally, "You want Lan to stay with us. Because she needs it, and because you hate losing people you promised to care for, especially children. Because too many under your responsibility have died. In the Court of Birth, and in Hawthorn." He reached out — unsure if that was even the right thing to do — and wrapped his hand around Asmodeus's own hand. Asmodeus didn't shake him off or pull away. Thuan squeezed, gently and carefully — and Asmodeus's face didn't move, but his entire posture relaxed.

"And you wouldn't necessarily mind a child, but you hate ghosts," Asmodeus said. He was silent, for a while. He shifted to look at Thuan, taking his glasses off and setting them on the bed. Without them, he looked young and vulnerable. "You believe the place of the dead isn't with the living."

"No," Thuan said. "That's not it. At least, not quite. Ghosts eat the living to remain in this world, and-—" He bit his lip. "I thought there was a choice between having her kill people, or having her feed on you. And she can't feed on you forever because she'll end up killing you, and I don't want to see you dead. I'm..." he stopped, heart hammering in his throat. If he didn't say it now, to his husband, who else was he going to say it to? "I'm scared I'll lose you. I almost did, with Khac Anh."

Asmodeus's eyes held him, light roiling in their depths. He laid a finger on Thuan's lips — held it there, pulsing with warmth, for a mere breath before taking it away. Thuan leant towards him, aching with need. "Oh, dragon prince. Haven't you worked it out by now?"

"What?" Thuan said.

"I'm *always* scared I'm going to lose you."

"You're not—" Thuan opened his mouth, closed it. He was going to protest that Asmodeus was never scared, but of course he was. Of course the sarcasm was nothing but a veneer to hide vulnerability — because to a Fallen who viewed threats and force as leverage to make people do what he wanted, what would his own fear be but a weakness to be hidden away?

"You care so little about yourself," Asmodeus said, shaking his head. "You want fairness and justice, but how fair are you being towards yourself?"

"That's not — I can't answer that truthfully."

A hint of laughter in Asmodeus's eyes. "No. It would probably not reflect well on you if you did."

Thuan said, finally — slowly, carefully, "You see a lot of yourself in Lan, don't you? A violent creature who'll kill to survive."

"Yes. And you thought Lan wasn't human. That she didn't deserve to live. It hurt." Asmodeus said, and stared back at Thuan levelly, grey eyes awash with worry. No sarcasm, no artifice: just sheer vulnerability.

Something twisted in Thuan's chest. Of course. That was why his rejection of Lan had been such a sore point — because if Thuan thought Lan was bloodthirsty and beyond Thuan's love, where would that leave Asmodeus?

But conversely — if Thuan could see and love Asmodeus, surely he could do the same with Lan. "I love you," he said, finally. "I know what you are and I love you. All of you."

Asmodeus's hand rested, gently, on his cheek. "Oh, dragon prince," he said. "And I you. Now and always."

"Asmodeus..." Thuan blinked furiously to clear the tears in his eyes.

"Ssh." Asmodeus's face was back to its usual mask. "Back to Lan. You said 'I thought' before. When you were talking about her."

"Well," Thuan said. He breathed out, slowly and carefully. "I asked Quang Thu. Lan needs blood. Not deaths."

"Ah." Asmodeus's face was oddly still. "And?"

"There's plenty of blood in the Hawthorn hospital," Thuan said. "As you well know. Some of it could even be yours, as long as you agree to not be the only donor. And if you let go of the bond between you."

A silence. Asmodeus watched him. Thuan knew he hated letting go — of things, of people, of failures. "A child," he said. "*Our* child."

A ghost. With fangs. And claws. And who couldn't speak, though they were going to teach her sign language, and Thuan was sure it wasn't going to take long. She was a fast learner. But, all the same, it would take a little while before he could get used to the idea. "You want her to stay. Lan wants to stay. And I... well, I've given it due thought," Thuan said.

"Have you?"

Thuan stared at him. "I know what you're doing. It's easier and more comfortable, isn't it, when we're not having a straight talk with each other. You're trying to rile me up so we'll be back to our old dynamics."

"It'd certainly be a great deal more comfortable if we were having a fight," Asmodeus said. "If less stable in the long run."

"Mmmph," Thuan said. "So?"

Another long, thoughtful silence. Then Asmodeus bent his head towards him — forehead gently touching the wood of Thuan's antlers, a soft, comforting roiling of Fallen magic that made Thuan feel light-headed and ready to burst. "We've come such a long way, haven't we, dragon prince." It was soft, without a trace of irony. Asmodeus's fingers gently ran through Thuan's hair, scattering hairpins on the floor, the same way he'd done in the abandoned shrine. Thuan trembled, caught in Asmodeus's firm grasp. "Let's see where this all goes, then."

Thuan reached out, and touched Asmodeus under his bare eyes — soft, short caresses that made Asmodeus's breath quicken. "Yes. Together," Thuan said, and drew his husband closer to him, and held him fast.

About the Author

Aliette de Bodard lives and works in Paris, where she has a day job as a System Architect. She studied Computer Science and Applied Mathematics, but moonlights as a writer of speculative fiction. Aliette has won three Nebula Awards, a Locus Award, a British Fantasy Award and four British Science Fiction Association Awards, and was a double Hugo finalist (Best Series and Best Novella).

Most recently she published *Fireheart Tiger* (Tor.com, Nebula Award finalist, British Science Fiction Association finalist), a sapphic romantic fantasy inspired by pre colonial Vietnam, where a diplomat princess must decide the fate of her country, and her own.

She is the author of the Dominion of the Fallen trilogy, set in a turn-of-the-century Paris devastated by a magical war–which comprises *The House of Shattered Wings* (Roc/Gollancz, 2015 British Science Fiction Association Award, Locus Award finalist), *The House of Binding Thorns* (Ace/Gollancz, 2017 European Science

Fiction Society Achievement Award, Locus award finalist), and *The House of Sundering Flames*.

Her short story collection *Of Wars, and Memories, and Starlight* is out from Subterranean Press.

She is also the author of *The Tea Master and the Detective* (2018 Nebula Award winner, 2018 British Fantasy Award winner, 2019 Hugo Award finalist), a murder mystery set on a space station in a Vietnamese Galactic empire, inspired by the characters of Sherlock Holmes and Dr. Watson; and *In the Vanishers' Palace*, a dark Beauty and the Beast retelling, where they are both women and the Beast is a dragon.

Visit her website www.aliettedebodard.com for free fiction (including further short stories set in the same universe as this one), Vietnamese and French recipes and more.

IN THE VANISHERS' PALACE

In a ruined, devastated world, where the earth is poisoned and beings of nightmares roam the land...

A woman, betrayed, terrified, sold into indenture to pay her village's debts and struggling to survive in a spirit world.

A dragon, among the last of her kind, cold and aloof but desperately trying to make a difference.

When failed scholar Yên is sold to Vu Côn, one of the last dragons walking the earth, she expects to be tortured or killed for Vu Côn's amusement.

But Vu Côn, it turns out, has a use for Yên: she needs a scholar to tutor her two unruly children. She takes Yên back to her home, a vast, vertiginous palace-prison where every door can lead to death. Vu Côn seems stern and unbending, but as the days pass Yên comes to see her kinder and caring side. She finds herself dangerously attracted to the dragon who is her master and jailer. In the end, Yên will have to decide where her own happiness lies—and whether it will survive the revelation of Vu Côn's dark, unspeakable secrets...

THE CITADEL OF WEEPING PEARLS

A Finalist for the 2015 Locus Award for Best Novella

The Citadel of Weeping Pearls was a great wonder; a perfect meld between cutting edge technology and esoteric sciences—its inhabitants capable of teleporting themselves anywhere, its weapons small and undetectable and deadly.

Thirty years ago, threatened by an invading fleet from the Dai Viet Empire, the Citadel disappeared and was never seen again.

But now the Dai Viet Empire itself is under siege, on the verge of a war against an enemy that turns their own mindships against them; and the Empress, who once gave the order to raze the Citadel, is in desperate needs of its weapons. Meanwhile, on a small isolated space station, an engineer obsessed with the past works on a machine that will send her thirty years back, to the height of the Citadel's power.

But the Citadel's disappearance still extends chains of grief and regrets all the way into the fraught atmosphere of the Imperial Court; and this casual summoning of the past might have world-shattering consequences...

FOR NEWS ABOUT JABBERWOCKY BOOKS AND AUTHORS

Sign up for our newsletter*: http://eepurl.com/b84tDz
visit our website: awfulagent.com/ebooks
or follow us on twitter: @awfulagent

THANKS FOR READING!

*We will never sell or give away your email address, nor use it for nefarious purposes. Newsletter sent out quarterly.